"Why don't you join me in the shower?" Sam offered.

"Yeah, right." Giselle laughed, running her fingers along his skin. "You just want me to wash your back."

"Hmm. My back wasn't exactly what I had in mind," he replied, nipping her neck.

She sucked in a quick breath. "Ah, a wicked mind. I like the way you think."

He licked the spot he'd just nipped. "Hey, I'm only thinking that you might have missed a few spots when you showered earlier," he said innocently. "Why don't you let me take care of them for you?" He reached behind the curtain and turned the water on. "It'll need a little time to warm up. What temperature do you prefer?"

"I like it hot," Giselle said, grinning. "Really, really hot."

"That's good. Then there's something for both of us." At her questioning look, he added,

"Because I like it wet…"

HIS CHRISTMAS FANTASY

BY
JENNIFER LaBRECQUE

 MILLS & BOON

First published in Great Britain 2009
Harlequin Mills & Boon Limited,
Eton House, 18-24 Paradise Road, Richmond, Surrey TW9 1SR

© Jennifer LaBrecque 2008

(Originally titled *Yule Be Mine*)

ISBN: 978 0 263 87500 3

14-1209

Harlequin Mills & Boon policy is to use papers that are natural, renewable and recyclable products and made from wood grown in sustainable forests. The logging and manufacturing processes conform to the legal environmental regulations of the country of origin.

Printed and bound in Spain
by Litografia Rosés S.A., Barcelona

After a varied career path that included barbecue-joint waitress, corporate numbers cruncher and bug-business maven, **Jennifer LaBrecque** has found her true calling writing contemporary romance. Named 2001 Notable New Author of the Year and 2002 winner of the prestigious Maggie Award for Excellence, she is also a two-time RITA® Award finalist. Jennifer lives in suburban Atlanta with one husband, one active daughter, one really bad cat, two precocious greyhounds and a chihuahua who runs the whole show.

To Girl: my daughter, my friend, my heart.

1

"WHEN ARE Helene and Mr. Wonderful getting here?" a muffled feminine voice asked as the kitchen door clicked closed behind Sam McKendrick, enveloping him in holiday scents of roasting turkey, pumpkin pie and fresh evergreen.

His sweeping glance, the practiced eye of a professional photographer, took in a green bean casserole in a glass dish waiting its turn in the oven, a mixing bowl surrounded by an opened bag of flour, measuring spoons and other baking paraphernalia on the yellow Formica countertop.

The crash and clang of falling pots and pans immediately followed from the lower corner cabinet where a very rounded rear was poking in the air, the speaker's top half swallowed by the cabinet. "Got it," the voice declared.

His new sister-in-law wiggled backward, freeing herself from the cabinet, an oversized cookie sheet in tow.

She straightened, stood, saw him and promptly dropped the cookie sheet. "Oh, hell." Within seconds, however, laughter offset the momentary consternation in her hazel eyes. "Mr. Wonderful, I presume."

Sam grinned. "Actually, it's McKendrick. Sam McKendrick. And you must be Giselle."

"Right." She glanced at the teakettle-shaped clock on the wall. "You're early."

Giselle Randolph was a hot mess.

Her long brown hair, caught up in a clip, stuck out at an odd angle on one side, and flour dusted the end of her freckled nose. She wore a white T-shirt with I Brake For Elves in green lettering across the front, a bright red, very sexy bra visible beneath the thin T-shirt and snug gray sweats. He noted her bare feet and red toenails, a green-and-white holly berry design detailed on each of her big toes.

Enchanting with an earthy sensuality, she was the sexiest woman he'd ever met, flour or no flour on her nose.

She quickly recovered her aplomb. She smiled, wiped her hand on her thigh and extended her hand in greeting. "Welcome to the family."

"Thanks." He shook her sticky hand and the oddest sensation zapped him, as if he'd just found something he hadn't known he was missing. Feeling slightly stunned, he shook his head to clear it and realized he was still engulfing her hand in his. He released her.

She grimaced an apology and wiped her hand ineffectually along the bottom of her T-shirt, which only tugged it tighter and threw her red plunging bra into further relief. "Sorry, didn't realize it was sticky." She waved her right hand, "Anyway…so, I guess I should thank you for eloping with my sister and saving me from some god-awful pink taffeta bridesmaid dress…or worse." She pretended to shudder.

"Glad I could help." He'd met Helene, a tall, cool blonde who turned heads everywhere she went, when she was on vacation at a resort in the Caymans and he was there shooting a brochure ad—not his typical assignment but he'd done it as a favor for his friend, who managed the resort. What followed was atypical, as well. Six whirlwind weeks and one Vegas elopement and honeymoon later and here he was, meeting the parents…and sister…on Christmas Day in suburban Atlanta.

"And my blushing-bride sister is where?"

"Your parents were out front working on the light display—"

She interrupted him, laughing. "More like fighting over the light display. You might as well get used to it. It's a ritual."

He laughed along with her, "Got it."

"Helene?" she prompted, as if she hadn't interrupted and he was the one who'd veered off topic. She retrieved the cookie sheet from the kitchen floor and put it on the counter.

"Talking to the next-door neighbors at the fence," he said before she cut him off again. "She sent me in with the luggage."

"Oh, right," she said, her expressive eyes widening as if she'd just noticed the rolling suitcase handle in his left hand and the travel bag slung over his shoulder. "Come on. I'll show you to Helene's old room."

He followed her down the hall of the rambling Victorian, which held a charming mix of antiques, clutter and Christmas decorations. They passed the front room, where a heavily decorated tree filled one corner and a cheery fire crackled in the fireplace. The setting could've been lifted from a made-for-TV Christmas special, a far cry from the public housing he'd grown up in. Buying his mother her own small house, complete with the white picket fence she'd longed for, had been one of the most satisfying moments of his life.

He started up the staircase, following Giselle, the stairs creaking loudly. Four steps up, he realized he was the only one setting them off. Giselle knew precisely where to place her foot to avoid the loud creak that seemed to come with every riser. He followed her lead, and there was no more creaking. She stopped and turned. Given the difference in their heights, it put them eye to eye.

"I see you've got it." She shook her head, smiling. "Once she started dating, Helene spent half her life grounded 'cause she'd get caught sneaking in late."

It was an amusing tidbit about his wife, but he found himself wondering about Giselle. "What about you?"

"I never snuck out." She was so close he didn't miss the flicker of wistfulness in her eyes. Her smile lit up her face, and he caught himself just in time from reaching out to wipe away the dusting of flour on her nose. "No one wanted to keep me out late the way they did Helene. You won't be surprised to know your wife always had the boys lined up."

"Not surprised at all. She's beautiful." Helene was beautiful. Sam realized he had a need, as a bastard kid

who'd grown up in public housing, to prove himself by
having the best. He might wear jeans, but his shirt was
always pressed and his jacket was Armani. His condo
downtown offered a great view of Atlanta's skyline. At
thirty, he was ready to settle down. Beautiful Helene
was a head-turner. He'd married her and committed to
a lifetime together, and Sam neither made nor took the
commitment lightly. Which was why he found it so
confounding to be standing on the stairs with his heart
slamming against his ribs and lost in the depths of
Giselle Randolph's hazel eyes.

"She is," Giselle said on a breathless note. Something real and hot and dangerous pulsed between them.
Something organic neither one had manufactured but
which they were both caught up in. She inhaled sharply,
and for one brief moment, like the slow descent of a
single drop of water captured on time-lapse film, she
leaned toward him. Her breath tumbled out in a sigh,
gusting warm and fragrant against his mouth.

Instinctively, he shifted toward her. The stair creaked
like a rifle shot, blasting away the intimacy and bringing
them both back to their senses.

She turned abruptly and led him up the stairs,
chatting as if that would erase whatever the hell had just
passed between them. "That's Mom and Dad's room at
the top of the stairs, so you can see how they were right
there to bust her. And then Daddy's study is off to the
right on the other side of their bedroom. My room is in
the attic. I talked the parental unit into letting me move
up there when I was twelve. It let my imagination run

free." That made sense. Helene had told him her sister was a writer. "And here's Helene's room...well, your room, too, now. Since you're married and all."

He deposited the suitcases at the foot of the bed as Giselle determinedly continued her tour guide monologue. "That's a picture of Helene when she won homecoming queen her junior year," she said, pointing to a particular picture in a wall full of framed glossies of his wife. "And that's when she was senior homecoming queen."

God, he wanted to kiss her to shut her up and, well, he just wanted to kiss her.

A sick feeling blossomed in his gut. Even further out of left field than the urge to kiss her came the traitorous thought that he'd up and married the wrong sister. And that was a helluva fix two days past his honeymoon.

The week before Christmas, two years later...

"HEY, GISELLE, got a minute?" Monica, *Life Trendz* magazine's editorial department secretary, stepped into Giselle's cubicle. "Change of plans on the Sedona trip."

Often the harbinger of less-than-stellar news, Monica had a the-shit's-about-to-hit-the-fan-but-don't-shoot-the-messenger smile she put on for such occasions. She wore that smile now.

"Sure." Trepidation crawled along Giselle's spine as she closed the file folder with her Sedona notes. She was flexible. Writing for a monthly magazine that covered recent innovations, new ideas, and current...well, trends demanded flexibility, but a change of plans on Friday when she was flying to Arizona on Sunday to start this project didn't sound promising. "What's up?"

"Do you want the good news or the bad news first?" Monica stepped into her cubicle but remained standing instead of making herself at home, the way she usually did in the folding chair shoved in one corner.

"Start with the bad so we can end on a positive note with the good."

"Darren's bagging the Sedona assignment."

"What? He can't do that." More than just the photographer she'd teamed up with for three years now, Giselle considered Darren a good friend. "Unless he has a really good reason, he's about to be a dead friend." She was only partially joking.

She stared at Monica and drummed her fingers on her desk, awaiting an explanation. "And by the way, he's a chicken to leave it up to you to tell me."

Monica offered a weak smile. "Something about him and Gerald and a progressive dinner and not having enough prep time if he goes."

"A progressive dinner?" Giselle shot to her feet. "That's it. He's dead. I'm going to kill him. I'll wait until after Christmas, but before the new year...."

"I know you've got a personal stake in this trip and you could've used Darren's moral support."

True enough, she had a personal stake in the Sedona assignment, but Monica was blissfully ignorant, as was everyone else other than Darren, as to the real reason behind her eagerness to cover the story. Writing for

Life Trendz meant sifting through scads of material for story ideas. She'd run across an online thread and *knew,* knew the moment she saw it, it was meant for her.

A New Age guru in Sedona claimed on the third day after the winter solstice, the shortest day of the year when the Earth rotated at its furthermost point from the sun in the northern hemisphere, there was an incredible spike at the energy vortexes in Sedona. Supposedly this surge at one particular vortex, which impacted both the male and female balance energies, had a profound effect on attractions and relationships. The guru claimed that couples who showed up there together tended to fall in love. There were even couples coming out for recommitment ceremonies, they were so convinced. Kind of a right-place-at-the-right-time love potion.

So, maybe it was a little out there, but that was the nature of most trends and the kind of stuff their readers loved. Giselle was willing to show up to see who else might be there, because anything was better than pining after a man you couldn't have and shouldn't want in the first place.

Monica, along with everyone else, thought her Sedona pilgrimage was to get over her ex-husband. They were wrong. Sam McKendrick was at the heart of her problem.

She'd never told anyone that running from her attraction to Sam was the real reason she'd married Barry Treadway. Except for her pathetic confession to Darren, over a shared pitcher of margaritas and chips and salsa in celebration of her divorce a couple of months ago. Darren, happy in his ten-year relationship with his partner Gerald and a romantic at heart, had proved an avid listener and sympathizer.

Once her Jose Cuervo buzz was gone, Giselle had sworn him to secrecy and forbidden him to bring it up again. She'd blabbed in a moment of weakness, but it wasn't something she wanted to run around discussing. It was bad enough suffering from infatuation-induced insanity without talking about it. She'd coined that catchy phrase herself by way of explaining why she, the responsible big sister who, despite the sibling rivalry that marked their relationship, generally adored her baby sister and always had her back, could fall into lust with Helene's husband.

From the moment she'd looked up in her mother's kitchen and seen Sam standing there…something had happened inside her. She'd fought it, run from it, tried to ignore it, but from the moment she'd laid eyes on Sam McKendrick, she'd wanted him. It wasn't as if she'd made the decision to want him. It was far worse. Something in her had responded to him, connected, and she'd been in a constant state of flux ever since.

Sam and Helene's whirlwind marriage had lasted a whopping eight months. Eight months before Sam had cheated on Helene. How could Giselle possibly still find herself hung up on a man who'd betrayed her sister? And the really pathetic part of her, the part she despised for even thinking such a thing, was furious that if he was going to cheat, she, Giselle, hadn't been an option. Not that she would have slept with her sister's husband, but…. And despite the knowing, despite the guilty sense of betrayal every time she thought of him, Sam McKendrick remained her forbidden fantasy.

She was resolute that this trip to Sedona would get her over Sam. It was meant to be, as if her stars were aligned just so. Darren bailing like this was merely a glitch, a minor hiccup.

Giselle started mentally running through the freelancers they'd used in the past. She'd be okay sharing a cottage with any of them. Apparently Sedona was the happening place at Christmas because Monica had had a heck of a time finding accommodations. She'd lucked out on a cancellation and managed to snag a two-bedroom cottage at a resort in the middle of Sedona. Serendipitous. Finding a sub willing to travel this close to Christmas would require one more dose of serendipity. She reached for her day planner.

"We'll just have to find a replacement," she said.

Monica stopped her. "That's the good news. Darren's already lined up his replacement."

"Good, maybe I won't kill him before New Year's Eve," Giselle said with a laugh. What was her problem? She should've known Darren wouldn't leave her hanging. Her problem was she was making herself crazy about this trip because she was so ready, okay, *desperate,* to get over Sam McKendrick. "It won't be the same as working with Darren because we're used to one another, but he wouldn't stick me with someone he didn't trust, especially on this assignment."

Monica stepped closer and cast a furtive glance about, as if Darren might be lurking in the potted plant down the hall. "Okay, he told me not to say anything," Monica said, lowering her voice, and Giselle bit back a smile. Darren knew that was a surefire way to get Monica to pass along the info. Monica liked being the one in the know. "But he says this guy is hot. And single. Oh, yeah, and straight," *definitely a salient point* "…you know, *available*. He said it was a shame to waste all that vortex voodoo."

Giselle perked up. Hope sprang eternal. Normally, she was the last person looking to be set up with someone, but if the guy was even halfway decent, and Darren tended to have excellent taste in men, she was more than happy to drag him along to the magic vortex with her. If she showed up with her own potential love match, then all the better to rid herself of her Sam McKendrick fixation.

It couldn't happen soon enough. Out of the blue, Sam had called. Two weeks ago she'd gotten home from work, and without any forewarning, she'd unsuspectingly punched the blinking button on her answering machine. She'd dropped her grocery bag and totally ruined a dozen eggs when she'd heard, "Giselle, this is Sam. I…uh…just wanted to touch base…maybe catch up. Call me."

Right. Maybe when hell froze over. She'd sunk to the sofa and hit the Repeat button and listened again, despising herself for her weakness, for the instant heat that rampaged through her at the mere sound of him, the way every cell in her body seemed to soak up the richness of his voice like a dry sponge in a spring rain. And then she'd leaned forward, her finger poised over the Delete button, and…she couldn't.

She still hadn't. But she would when she got home today. This time she really would. And she wouldn't hit Play and listen *again* before she deleted it. Yep, Sedona was all about healing and starting over—that had to be why she'd found the online thread two days after Sam's phone call—and if she happened to haul along her own potential candidate, where was the harm?

Hope and enthusiasm buoyed Giselle's mood. "Hot, single, and available—what's not to love?"

Monica beamed in relief and waved her hand. "And Darren was all worried you'd be pissed."

"I prefer him because I'm used to him, but if he's lined up a decent photographer who's all of the above, I'm good with that."

As a general rule, men didn't fall all over themselves around Giselle. She'd grown up the brains, her sister the beauty. Giselle took too much after her father's side of the family to be a man-magnet, but hey, with all the energy and stuff floating around Sedona, who knew? Anything was possible, wasn't it?

"Darren says this guy's dropping by around," Monica checked her watch, "well, *now,* to go over the assignment particulars with you." She rubbed her hands together in anticipation. "I can't wait to get a look at him. In fact, I think I'll have lunch at my desk so I can check out your new love slave." She did a Groucho

Marx waggle of her eyebrows. "That is what this vortex thing is going to do, right? Turn him into your personal love slave?"

Giselle laughed, more excited than ever. She had a funny feeling in her tummy, a *knowing*, all doubts gone. This trip was about to change her life.

"I'll let you know when I get back." She picked up her note file from her desk.

Monica turned to leave. Giselle stopped her, grabbing a pen. "Wait a sec. I can probably figure it out on my own since good-looking strangers don't drop by my home-away-from-home cube every day, but does this camera-carrying paragon of manliness have a name? He probably won't answer to love slave until after we get to Sedona." She was terrible with names. This way she wouldn't have to stress about remembering his when they met if she already had it written down. She flipped open the file folder, ready to jot his name on the inside flap.

Monica wrinkled her nose and Giselle laughed.

"You're just creating a cheat sheet," Monica accused. Okay, everyone in the department knew Giselle was bad with names. "Sam McKendrick. But he might like it if you call him Love Slave."

Giselle swayed on her feet and for a second thought she might pass out. No, no, no! Anyone. Anybody. Just not *him*. "Son of a bitch," she wailed. "No!"

Darren was deader than dead.

As if conjured from the depths of hell or every fantasy she'd had for the last two years, the devil himself sauntered into her cubicle. A laconic smile crinkled the corners of his hooded blue eyes. Stubble shadowed his rugged jaw and his dark brown hair looked as if he'd run his fingers, rather than a comb, through it. He'd paired a crisp white collared shirt with a well-cut jacket and jeans. Just as she remembered him. Equally familiar, her pulse raced and an illicit tingling raced through her body, leaving frantic heat in its wake.

Sam.

Her folder and pen slipped through her hands; papers scattered across the floor.

"I thought I heard my name, but just for the record, Love Slave works for me."

2

SAM TOOK her *son of a bitch* and my-worst-nightmare-just-walked-through-the-door expression as good signs. If she was that emphatic, that reactive, then Darren was right and she was interested.

"It's been a long time, Giselle."

She knelt to gather her papers. "Not long enough, Sam," she said, but scrambling around on the floor sort of ruined her haughty tone.

He squatted to help, bringing him that much closer to her. He breathed in her scent and drank in the sight of her. Despite the passage of time and all the water under their respective bridges, he felt the impact of her in his gut, the same as he had the first time he'd met her. Back then, she'd worn her brown hair long and pulled up in a clip. Now she sported a sleek chin-length bob with red highlights. "I like your hair, it suits you."

"That's a load off my mind," she said without looking at him. She leaned forward to pick up the last piece of paper but he beat her to it. He held it out. Her eyes met his, and the rest of the world faded to nothingness. Once again, he was lost in those hazel eyes, and despite her sarcasm he recognized the flare of desire in their depths.

"Obviously, you've met before," the other woman in the cubicle said, jerking him back to the rest of the world. Sam had forgotten she was there.

He stood and slipped his hand beneath Giselle's elbow to help her up. She straightened, shrugging off his touch. His gut knotted from just that brief contact with her.

He turned to the other woman and extended his hand. "Sam McKendrick, Giselle's new love slave."

The woman snickered. Giselle glared.

She shook his hand. "Monica Dixon, department secretary extraordinaire."

Monica Dixon radiated curiosity.

"Sam was my sister Helene's first husband," Giselle said.

Clean, simple, straightforward. She deliberately ignored his love slave reference.

"Your ex-brother-in-law? No kidding. Small world." Monica looked from him to Giselle and shrugged. "At least it's not your ex-husband. *That* would be uncomfortable."

"The ninth ring of hell," Giselle said.

Hot damn! She wasn't pining for Barry post-divorce. The guy had never been right for her. Standing by and watching Giselle marry a man who was obviously all wrong for her, who didn't appreciate her, was one of the hardest things Sam had ever done. But he'd been married to Helene and there'd been no other option, no other choice. *Now* was a whole new ball game. Sam was single and, according to Darren, as of mid-September, so was Giselle. "I heard you and Barry had split."

Monica backed out of the cubicle opening. "I'll just leave the two of you to play catch-up and sort things out. I'm going to lunch."

Giselle slanted her an amused glance. "I thought you were skipping lunch today."

The woman offered a conspiratorial smile. "Not now. See ya."

Obviously an inside joke.

Giselle turned to face him, her hair framing her face. Her earlier amusement disappeared, leaving her hazel eyes curiously flat.

"I don't want to work with you," she said, crossing her arms over her rounded breasts, which were impossible to ignore in a curve-hugging T-shirt beneath her well-cut pantsuit jacket. He'd never forgotten that red bra beneath her white T-shirt when he first met her. Forget, hell. He thought of it often. Was she wearing a red bra beneath her T-shirt now?

"Really? And I thought son of a bitch was an exclamation of delight." He propped himself against the other end of her desk. "Why wouldn't you want to work with me? I'm very good at what I do."

"Maybe I object on moral grounds."

"We're mature adults. I'm sure we can both make it through four days and remain civil and professional."

Any further objections on her part would paint her as being immature and unprofessional. He'd learned at an early age that you couldn't wait for life to hand you things. If you wanted something, you worked your ass off and made it happen. He'd worked hard at school and a career that took him far from the housing projects he'd grown up in. But it was true enough that you could take the man out of the projects but you could never take the projects out of the man. Sam would never be content to sit back and take what life gave him. He wanted Giselle. He would've never, ever approached her as long as either of them were married, but now he wanted to see if there might be something there, if what he'd felt the first time he saw her, if what he sensed from her was real.

She narrowed her eyes, fully realizing he'd just backed her into a corner and thrown down the gauntlet. Meeting his challenge head-on, she set her chin at a determined angle. "Fine. I'll e-mail you the briefing notes this afternoon. I've got a few updates." Her lips tightened, precisely the same way Helene's did when she was pissed. "Since we're discussing professionalism, we're sharing a two-bedroom cottage. I'd prefer you not entertain while we're there."

"I think I can manage. It's not as if I keep a harem."

"You did while you were married." She lobbed the accusation at him.

He took the hit. He'd wondered how long it would take her to bring it up. Less than fifteen minutes. One drunk night. One woman. One big-ass mistake. Getting drunk had not been the best response to finding a guy in *his* bed with *his* wife.

Had Helene told her family she'd been sleeping with

not just any guy but Sam's best friend for months before he found them in bed together? Probably not. And it didn't really matter because it didn't exonerate him. Sleeping with a stranger because he was angry and hurt had been wrong. And playing the blame game accomplished nothing.

"Hardly a harem. But to put your mind at ease, I'm not going there to look for another woman. I will, of course, expect the same courtesy from you."

For a moment she looked startled, as if she hadn't expected that. "Not a problem. You know Helene's remarried." She relayed the news, ever the big sister. It had shades of the day she'd pointed out Helene's homecoming accomplishments.

"Of course I know." He laughed. "Danny was still mid-proposal when she phoned to tell me."

Giselle didn't appreciate his dry sense of humor. "She's very happy now."

"That's a relief."

She narrowed her eyes at him, again—she had the eye-narrowing down to a fine art. She'd mistaken his comment for sarcasm. Although he wasn't happy that Helene had slept around on him with his best friend, and God knows he still missed Danny, Sam had known their marriage was over before then. After his initial bout of anger, he'd realized he was actually relieved that their mistake of a marriage *was* over.

Giselle ignored his comment and shoved her laptop into a padded carrier. "I need your e-mail to forward the project outline."

He plucked a business card from his jacket pocket and handed it to her. "I'm looking forward to Sedona."

She took the card, not touching him in the exchange, and dropped it in her laptop satchel. "So am I." She offered him a smile he thought was meant to be professional but came across as slightly grim. "I'll send the file later."

She slung her handbag over her shoulder and he stepped out of her cubicle ahead of her, into the hallway. "Thanks. I'll see you Sunday."

He turned on his heel and made his way down the hall toward the elevators. What he wanted to do was the same thing he'd wanted to do since the first time he met her. He wanted to pull her into his arms, bury his hands in her hair, kiss her senseless and then make love to her until she couldn't remember her own name.

That, however, would have to wait another few days. But it would happen. He'd come for her and he was ready to lay siege.

GISELLE LOCKED the doors of her VW Bug and collapsed against the upholstered seat, determined to pull herself together. The parking garage's top deck was mercifully deserted on the Friday before Christmas. Lots of people must have left work early to shop, or they were taking the following week off and had gotten a head start, she absently speculated.

She welcomed the car's near-freezing temperature. She felt hot and confused and generally a mess. Gray clouds covered the sky like a woolen winter blanket. They seemed somewhat appropriate.

She fished her cell phone out of her satchel, scrolled through the stored names and hit the speed dial.

"Do you know why I'm calling?" Giselle asked without preamble, speaking into her hands-free set even though she was still sitting in her parked car. She didn't dare drive during this conversation. She'd probably crash. Not that she had anywhere to go. She'd just wanted to get rid of Sam before she did something stupid like step between his splayed legs, wrap her arms around his neck and give in to the plaguing temptation to discover what his mouth felt like against hers, how he tasted and just how good it might feel to have all of his parts close to all of her parts that tingled and throbbed for his touch.

That, however, might send a mixed signal following her declaration that she didn't want to work with him or even talk to him. Although what she had in mind wasn't technically working or even talking. Moaning and heavy breathing did not conversation make.

Not to mention that if it did happen, news would spread through the entire office in a heartbeat. And last, but definitely not least, she would never be able to face her family afterward and live with herself.

All in all, getting him out of her office had been the better plan.

"You're calling to thank me for being a good friend?" Darren said.

Giselle snapped.

"What were you thinking? What did you tell him? Oh, and remind me to never split a pitcher of margaritas with you again. Ever. And you are a major chicken-shit that you didn't tell me this to my face." She finally ran out of steam and ended her rant.

"Relax. I was subtle."

Yeah. Darren was to *subtle* what she was to beauty-queen *beautiful.* Giselle groaned. "There's nothing subtle about you."

"I called him under the guise of talking about a couple of his pieces in a small gallery, you know, one photographer to another. I hadn't even gotten around to working you into the conversation when *he* brought you up."

"He brought me up?" she echoed rather stupidly, her pulse moving into overdrive. She idly smoothed her hand over the gearshift's rounded knob.

"Apparently he recognized my name and knew I worked with you. Said he reads the magazine. He asked about you. I mentioned the divorce, yada, yada, yada, he asked for your number."

A raindrop splattered against her windshield. Then another and another.

"He called and left a message a couple of weeks ago," she told him.

"Let me guess, you didn't call him back." Giselle could practically see his eyes roll.

It began to rain in earnest. "What was the point? My intention is to get over him, not talk to him."

"Did you ever think, Girl Genius, that talking to him, going on assignment with him is just the way to do that?"

"Actually, no. It strikes me as dangerously stupid." Case in point: she'd told Sam she didn't want to work with him. That was the sensible, cautious side of her. However, there was a part of her deep down inside that wanted to give in to the opportunity to spend four torturous days with him. In the last half hour, she'd felt more alive, more tuned in to everything, as if she'd finally fully awakened since…well, the last time she was around Sam McKendrick. What she felt around Sam was what she'd *wanted* to feel when she'd married Barry—an electric sizzle, an almost frantic compulsion to touch and be touched, a restless ache deep inside that seemed an instinctive response to *him*.

She slammed the lid shut on that Pandora's box. Not only had Sam been her sister's husband, he'd cheated on Helene. Strictly off limits. Verboten.

Frustration welled inside her, a countermeasure to her incendiary sexual response to Mr. Wrong. "Riddle me this. How am I supposed to get over him when he's right frickin' there?"

"Selle, honey, haven't you ever been shopping, seen a wickedly expensive dress and known that even if you were willing to eat beans for the next two months, you still couldn't have that dress?"

"Um…no. I don't really wear dresses," she said, "so I've never been in that situation." He deserved a dose of obtuse.

Darren offered a long-suffering sigh. "For hypothetical situations, we're going to pretend you have. What should you do?"

He loved constructing these little illustrative vignettes. What the hell, she'd play along. He usually made a point…sooner or later. "Walk away and look for a knockoff I can afford in another store."

"That's your first mistake." Darren pounced on her. "And that's why you wound up with a man who didn't suit you. You settled."

"Sometimes you're amazingly insightful."

"I know." She sensed his grin on the other end. "What you need to do is march into that store and try on the dress. You *always* try it on and then when it doesn't look as good as it should on your bodacious self for that kind of money, you can walk away from it feeling good about not buying it."

The idea of "trying on" Sam instantly gave her a mental image of the two of them engaged in hot, sweaty sex, which actually was a mental image that was never very far away. "I'm not *trying him on*."

"I didn't mean literally…although that could work. I meant that if you spend a couple of days with him, you might find out you don't really like him." She heard Gerald's voice in the background. "Hold on a sec," Darren said to her, and then he was talking to Gerald. "Yeah, I'm almost through. I'm talking Giselle off a ledge."

She snorted in his ear. "Humph. Talking yourself out of hot water is more like it." He laughed, and she continued, "And what if you try on the dress and it looks even better than you thought and you still can't have it?"

"You're screwed." He didn't have to sound so cheery about it. "But at least you can admire the way you look in it for a few minutes. Or sell your soul to the devil and buy it anyway."

"That's so helpful…and reassuring."

"I'm always here for you, hon. Listen, gotta run. Give me a call when you get back and you can thank me then."

"Or not. I'd suggest you spend the next few days getting your affairs in order," she suggested darkly.

Another laugh, followed by, "Ta," and Darren was gone.

Giselle disconnected the call on her end. She tucked the phone back into her case and watched the rain form rivulets on her windshield. She still didn't know how Sam had wound up on this assignment. And it didn't really matter, did it?

Come hell or high water, she was getting over Sam on this trip. The alternative wasn't an option.

3

GISELLE SHIFTED in her aisle seat on Sunday morning as the non-stop Atlanta-to-Phoenix flight continued to board.

Sam had arrived. She sensed him, felt him, as if she was tuned in to him on a level she'd never experienced with anyone else. She looked up from her magazine and her breath caught in her throat as her eyes met his. He just looked so…well, damn glad to see her. The kind of look lovers would share on a crowded plane.

And then he was there, beside her.

"Worried I wouldn't make it?" Sam said by way of greeting. His cocky grin, however, carried an edge of uncertainty.

"One can always hope." Instead of coming out crisp and biting as she'd intended, she sounded breathless and teasing, undone by that combination of smile and faint hesitation, as if it actually mattered to him whether she was glad to see him or not. And once again she was disgusted with herself that even though he was a cheating bastard, his blue eyes still set her heart tripping.

Giselle had arrived at the airport early enough to grab a coffee and bagel and skim the morning newspaper before she was called to board the flight from Atlanta to Phoenix. Arriving early hadn't been a problem since she'd tossed and turned all night—yet another sleepless night compliments of Sam McKendrick.

She really hadn't been sure Sam would show at all. But there he stood, larger than life.

Stepping closer to her aisle seat, he hoisted his equipment bag into the overhead bin, which was all good and fine except it put his other equipment right at eye level.

Look away, look away, look away, she told herself, but somewhere along the route to her brain her libido intercepted the message and she continued to stare at his crotch, the bulge between his thighs thrown into relief by his upraised arms. Finally, he settled his carry-on and she hastily averted her eyes, which did nothing to abate the heat radiating from her core. One lousy Sam's-crotch-at-her-eye-level encounter and it was as if a furnace switch had been flipped on inside her.

"Want to move over?"

He wished. "No. I don't." She smiled and stood, stepping out into the aisle. She always requested the aisle seat. A blonde who'd given Giselle a dismissing look earlier sat next to the window. Giselle hated being squashed into the center seat. She offered Sam a bright smile. "I believe you're in the middle."

Karma was a bitch. Going to Sedona, doing this story, this was her big chance to get over this…ridiculous…

making-her-crazy…*thing* she had for Sam. This was supposed to be her cure, her fix. And then he'd ruined it by showing up. Of all the assignments to get—him… now. Seemed sort of fitting he had to scrunch his six-foot plus, broad-shouldered, long, muscular-legged, crotch-bulging—self into the center seat. Served him right for plaguing her.

She extended her two hands, palms up, the way they did on game shows when they were showcasing a prize. "Enjoy." She offered an evil smirk.

His blue eyes twinkled and she wanted to kick herself. She was aiming for hateful, at least sarcastic, and he seemed to think she was flirting with him. She wasn't flirting. Nope. Because that would be like ducking under a line of yellow tape with Warning Do Not Cross in big bold black letters.

"Okay, then." He slid in, folding himself into the tight spot.

Giselle sat back down and her space shrank proportionately to accommodate Sam next to her. Short of leaning out into the aisle, she couldn't get away from his broad shoulder against hers. Her stomach somersaulted, and she felt even more flushed than when she'd been face to crotch two minutes ago. He dug around and clicked his seat belt into place, his muscles bunching against her arm as he completed the simple task.

And he smelled…well, good, dammit. Not that she wanted to be stuck next to him for the next four hours if he had body odor or halitosis, but she didn't need this, either. His scent was fresh and clean, like that of a man just out of the shower with the faint blend of soap, deodorant and a hint of mint toothpaste. Enticing. Appealing. Arousing.

No doubt about it, karma was definitely a bitch. And she was paying for having developed a crush on her sister's husband the first time she laid eyes on him and for wanting him from then to now and all the stinking time in between and for still feeling this horrible tingly, I'm-so-alive feeling when she was around him, even though she knew he was a cheat and she was a sick puppy to still feel that way. Yes, she was being punished.

He turned his head to face her. They were close enough she could see her reflection in his eyes. It was like being enveloped in a blanket of Sam, of forbidden want. Forget it. She wasn't being punished. She was being tortured.

"I read through your notes and the article outline last night," he said. "I wanted to bounce a couple of ideas off you."

She and Darren often spent a flight brainstorming. It was the perfect use of time. She occasionally talked to other people on board when she traveled alone. But it had never felt like this—dangerously intimate, as if she couldn't quite catch her breath. As if she was rather rapidly losing her mind....

If Sam leaned just a little closer to her, and she a little closer to him...his mouth, with that sensually full lower lip, was right there. Never once when she and Darren were seated next to one another had such errant thoughts run through her head.

She looked away from him and blindly reached out to straighten the magazine and paper stuffed in the seat back in front of her. And no, it wasn't to occupy her hands with something other than cupping his jaw. Well, maybe it was. "I'd rather talk about it on the drive up from Phoenix," she said.

Discussing a project with him that centered on falling in love seemed a much safer proposition with the rental car's front seat between them. She really looked at the seatback ahead of her and realized she'd just rearranged the barf bag. Kind of fitting, actually.

He shrugged and the movement echoed through her as his shoulder rubbed against her. "Sure. However you want to play it."

She picked up her magazine and proceeded to ignore him. Or rather, she tried. Sam wasn't an easy man to ignore. He wasn't loud or boisterous or ultrahigh-energy. If anything, he tended to be on the quiet side, a man comfortable in his own skin who didn't need to be the constant center of attention. But he radiated a strength and determination, a grit that gave him presence.

She was conscious of him on every level—his scent, his arm resting near hers, the hug of worn denim across his thighs, his broad, well-shaped hands, the smattering of dark hair beneath the pressed cuff of his white shirt—the same as Christmas night two years ago.

That had the dubious distinction of being both the best night of her life and the worst, both exhilarating and mortifying. She recalled it with such clarity that it could have been last night rather than two years ago.

They'd feasted on Christmas dinner and retired to the parlor so Dad could watch The History Channel. Sam, Helene and Giselle had headed over to the love seat to finish off a leftover bottle of zinfandel. Giselle was glad, really she was, when Helene had settled herself on Sam's lap. They were newlyweds and Giselle was thrilled to see her sister so happy. They'd only polished off half a glass of wine when their mother had called Helene over to look at kitchen remodeling magazines. Mom's kitchen was definitely long overdue. Giselle did not, however, possess Helene's knack for interior design, which left her sharing the love seat with her new brother-in-law.

The Christmas tree lights were winking and blinking, a dying fire glowed in the fireplace, and Giselle, who'd been on guard all day against any more errant moments such as the one on the stairs when she'd been showing Sam to Helene's room, foolishly relaxed. She and Sam talked writing and photography and argued whether the Cubs or Braves had a better pennant chance in the upcoming year.

Sam had laughed at something she said and in that instant everything shifted, tangled, clarified. The most intense surge of sexual longing had ripped through her, shaken her to her core. She'd wanted to use her hands and mouth to map the angles of his face, the rugged line of his jaw, the broad expanse of his chest, his slightly splayed thighs and all the areas in between.

It didn't matter that her family sat a stone's throw away in the same room. She'd ached for the press of his body, the slide of his hands beneath her clothes, on her bare flesh. She'd wanted to taste him, feel him, every intimate inch. Like a flash flood roaring through a dry canyon, desire had deluged her. The intensity was a hundred times what it had been earlier on the stairs.

He was her sister's husband. She'd excused herself posthaste and all but run to her room. She'd felt ridiculous, guilty and horrified that Sam or any of her family might've had any inkling of the direction of her thoughts. And while she'd hid in her room, she couldn't escape the unquenched fire that followed her.

She'd made sure she was out the door and on a long walk bright and early the next morning when Helene and Sam were leaving. She'd vowed to keep away from him. She'd be pleasant but distant. And still her feelings plagued her for days, weeks, months. Sam became her forbidden fantasy.

She'd never felt so damn guilty in her life because not only was Sam her sister's husband, but she'd known, for that moment in time, that Sam wanted her in return. She'd felt the impact of his gaze lingering on her lips and knew he wanted her, and she was so ashamed that she'd known not only the sweet, hot ache of physical desire but a flare of triumph that he wanted *her,* Giselle. Wrong, wrong, wrong on so many levels. It wasn't Helene's fault that men had always been attracted to her, rather than Giselle, the sister with the good personality. Nor was it Helene's fault that the boy Giselle had such a horrible crush on in high school had asked to walk Giselle home…just to wangle an introduction to her sister.

And there'd been something so noble in the fact that Sam had looked away first. If she had to feel this betraying lust, this forbidden desire for her sister's husband, at least he was worthy of the guilt Giselle felt for coveting him. And of course, she'd never actually betray Helene by doing anything, and neither would Sam. That had been apparent. And somewhere in there the illicit attraction she felt for him was compounded by a sense of sacrifice. She might want him, and he might have wanted her, but they'd both looked away because it was the right thing to do.

And then she'd found out he'd betrayed Helene and it had been doubly painful. Not only was he not the noble man she'd thought him, but his affair with some nameless woman meant he'd looked at someone else the way he'd looked at Giselle, with that same yearning, and it had rendered that night meaningless, robbed it of its magic.

She should've thanked him for that. For turning her something-beyond-infatuation into loathing. But then that loathing became self-loathing because even though he wasn't worthy, even though he was a cheat, she couldn't seem to scour him from her mind.

And now, mind aside, he was seated next to her on her pilgrimage to get over him once and for all. And the truly wretched part was that if he stood up right now and announced he wasn't going and walked off the plane, she was fairly certain she'd be more mournful than celebratory. *Oh, what a tangled web...*

She felt him look at her, but she steadfastly pretended to read her magazine, turning a page for good measure. She felt too raw, too vulnerable to risk glancing at him.

To Sam's right, the blonde all but leaned into his lap, or maybe she was just carried by the momentum of her oversized boobs.

"Hi, I'm Felicity," she said, introducing herself to Sam. "Are you two together?" Felicity's voice grated, painfully perky after Giselle's near-sleepless night.

Giselle kept her eyes trained on the magazine page in front of her, but she felt Sam's quick glance in her direction. "We're coworkers. This is a business trip."

"What kind of business are you in?"

Giselle retrieved her iPod from where she'd stored it in the seat back ahead of her.

"I'm a photographer and Giselle's a journalist. We're working on a magazine article."

"Ohh," Felicity squealed. "A photographer. How fascinating."

Giselle shoved in her earphones and turned the unit on. She'd flown often enough to zone out the flight attendants upcoming safety spiel. She'd rather be nibbled to death by vampire ducks than listen to Felicity flirt with Sam the entire trip. Thanks, however, to her foresight in charging her iPod, vampire ducks were totally unnecessary.

The opening chords of Ravel's "Bolero" swelled in her ears, muting Sam's low rumble and Felicity's *enthusiastic* response. She closed her eyes, giving herself over to the music's passion and sensuality.

She still sensed his body heat, the proximity of his leg, arm and shoulder. There was no escaping the subtle combination of soap and maleness that was Sam, but at least without seeing him and hearing him she hoped to maintain a little distance…and sanity.

Sam McKendrick was a sickness…and she desperately needed a cure.

SAM EMBRACED the silence filling the car as they left the remnants of suburban Phoenix behind and headed north on Route 17 to Sedona.

Giselle drove the rental SUV. It was her story, her project, and she wasn't a woman who would put him behind the wheel of the car simply because he was a man. That was fine with him. He studied her profile as she navigated a lane change.

His ex-wife and her mother boasted classically beautiful features of high, sculpted cheekbones, flawless complexions, straight noses, thick curling lashes surrounding slightly exotic eyes, and lush full mouths. Giselle, however, had inherited the Randolph features. Her small, slightly snub nose bore a liberal sprinkling of freckles; her cheeks were more round than angular; wispy lashes framed her hazel eyes; and although well-shaped, her mouth lacked the pouting fullness of her mother's and sister's. However, Giselle exuded an innate sensuality.

It was as if Helene was so used to her looks commanding attention that she'd never bothered to develop any other attributes, whereas Giselle immersed herself in the world around her and it filtered back through her, lending her a depth and earthy sexiness his ex-wife didn't possess.

"What?" She slanted him a brief look and then trained her eyes once again on the road. "Don't stare at me."

"I wasn't staring, I was looking." He couldn't seem to get enough of looking at her.

"Well, don't. Don't look at me." Her rigid shoulders and faint frown screamed *Off Limits*.

"Why not?" He ignored her off-limits order. "I like looking at you."

She in turn pretended she hadn't heard his declaration. If he hadn't been watching so closely, he would've missed her almost imperceptible gasp. "It makes me nervous and you should never make the driver nervous."

"Is it me in particular or people in general looking at you that rattles you? Most women like being looked at," he said. Helene had seemed to crave it, in fact.

"I'm not most women," she said on a husky note, "so you can stop."

No. She definitely wasn't most women. She was smart, sexy and slightly bohemian. She defied categorizing, which was why he hadn't been able to forget her. What would she say if he told her he wanted to do so much more than simply look at her? He wanted to kiss her until she forgot that he'd once been married to her sister and that her entire family despised him. He wanted to hear her gasp with pleasure.

"I'm a slave to your happiness. Your wish is my

command." His rejoinder hung between them, bound them, thickening the air with a raw sexual awareness. An image clicked into his head like a film frame. Giselle naked in his bed, her sweet nipple in his mouth, his cock buried deep inside her, his hand between them, stroking her clit as he dedicated himself to bringing her to orgasm.

Color stained her face, as if she knew what he was thinking. "Then you should've stayed home, Sam."

Rather than any real venom, he thought he detected a desperate note in her rebuttal. Or maybe he was just projecting his own sense of desperation in taking the assignment so he could see her again.

"It's a little late for me to stay home. Plus I'd miss seeing this part of the country."

"Then try looking out the window," she said dryly.

He laughed because that was definitely the Giselle he knew and he was just damn glad to be here, sharing a ride with her. "Fine. You drive and I'll watch the scenery."

He unzipped the equipment bag he'd stored on the floorboard and pulled out his camera. Even when he wasn't looking at her, she seemed to surround him.

In his mind, he slid the straps of that red bra down her shoulders, his fingers dragging along the soft warmth of her skin. Where did her freckles end? What did her breasts look like without her bra? Prominent or small nipples? Rose-hued or darker, duskier? Was she a pubic waxing fanatic or was she more *au naturel?*

He didn't need to be thinking about her naked, or it

could be damn embarrassing when it was time to get out of the car or if she happened to glance over and down.

He spent a few minutes adjusting the settings, cleaning the lens, and then resolutely looked out the passenger window. On both sides of the divided highway, towering saguaro cactus dotted the arid brown landscape like green giants. "It is spectacular, isn't it?"

"It must've been something to travel through here by stagecoach back in the day," Giselle said, her voice low and reflective.

"Yeah. Hot in the summer, cold in the winter."

"Very funny." Amusement sparkled in her eyes and he knew a moment of intense satisfaction that he'd been responsible for putting it there.

Wind gusted through the canyon and buffeted the SUV. "And windy."

"Obviously you're not channeling the pioneering spirit."

He grinned at her dry wit, one of the things he'd liked so much about her from the beginning. "'Fraid not."

"So you had some ideas you wanted to bounce around on the article?"

He might've railroaded his way into this assignment, but they still needed to be on the same page with the article. When a writer and a photographer "spoke" at cross-purposes it resulted in substandard work. Sam didn't do substandard.

He'd resolved as a kid that if people wanted to slap a label on him, he'd make damn sure that label was

Excellence. He demanded it of himself and expected it from others, as well.

"So, the way I understand it from your outline, there's an urban legend taking shape that couples who show up at this particular vortex on the third day after the winter solstice fall in love."

"There's a little more to it than that, but that's the gist of it. You don't actually have to be a couple. Singles apparently show up there," she shrugged, "and sometimes the magic works and sometimes it doesn't."

"Sounds like the power of suggestion to me. It's hard to believe someone falls in love because of winter solstice at a Sedona vortex. That just seems like a lot of hocus-pocus, but I'll still be glad to take photos."

"So you don't believe in magic?"

He leaned into the space between them, narrowing the distance. He caught another whiff of her perfume. If scents were translated to pictures, this one evoked a dark, erotic blend of swirls and curves in shades of ruby red and purple against a blanket of yellow-gold. Complex and evocative beneath the surface. It suited her. "Do *you* believe in magic?"

"I trust you're a better photographer than you are interviewer."

He chuckled. "Am I interviewing you?"

"If you were, you'd be doing a lousy job. You're obviously biased."

"And you're hedging." She was a crafty one, Giselle was. "Do you believe in magic?"

"I believe in forces of energy we can't necessarily see."

Forces of energy. Something stirred inside him, a resonance, an acknowledgement. "I take it that's a yes. Have you ever experienced magic yourself?"

Her hands tightened on the wheel and he felt her hesitation, as if she might refuse to answer. She was right. He was a lousy interviewer. She tilted her chin up. "Maybe…once…I'm not sure, but it doesn't mean it doesn't exist."

Gooseflesh prickled his skin and the first time he ever saw her came to mind, swiftly followed by that Christmas night two years ago. Forces of energy. That summed it up exactly.

He asked the question that had been bugging him ever since he'd skimmed Darren's assignment notes. "Are you coming with a personal interest? Are you looking to fall in love?"

"It crossed my mind." Her smile had an edge to it. "Who couldn't use some help in their love life?"

That made him want to grind his teeth. "Come on. You're writing this story, but you don't really believe this, do you?"

"How are you so sure it's not real?"

"It's not an issue for me. I can take the photos all day long but it doesn't mean I believe this magic nonsense."

Before she could respond, a massive wind gust barreled through the canyon. One minute they were driving along in their lane and the next a trailer swaying behind a pickup in the lane beside them bounced off the SUV, metal screeching against metal, sending them spinning out of control.

4

"ARE YOU okay?" Sam's voice came to her as if it were muffled by fog. "Giselle?" His urgent tone snapped her out of what must have been mild shock.

"Yeah. Yeah, I'm fine. You?"

"I'm good."

They sat on the shoulder of the road, the SUV's motor still running, the vehicle upright but facing oncoming traffic. Adrenaline kicked in. Her heart pounded. Her hands shook. "What the hell just happened?"

Sam raked an unsteady hand through his hair. "The wind blew that trailer into us, they sideswiped us and kept going. Nice job of handling the car, by the way."

Giselle laughed abruptly. "I didn't handle anything. I just held on to the wheel and it was all a blur."

"Exactly. We'd have rolled if you'd overreacted and tried to fight it." He released his seat belt. "Sit tight. I'll check out the damage to the vehicle. We may have to report it as a hit-and-run for the insurance to cover it."

Sam opened his door and cold wind whistled into the car. Giselle tugged her down vest tighter about her while he climbed out and rounded the front of the vehicle. She powered down her window and stuck her head out into the bracing December air, expecting to see dents and scrapes along her side. *Nothing.* She blinked. Nothing marred the white paint along the entire driver's side. Sam moved to stand beside her door.

"Am I missing something here?" She looked up at Sam. "Are you *not* seeing the same thing I'm *not* seeing?"

He dropped to his haunches and ran his hand lightly over the front panel and her door. "No dents. No scrapes. Not even a scratch." He slowly stood up.

"But that trailer hit us…I heard it…felt it…how can…."

"I don't know." Sam skirted the vehicle again and climbed back in.

"That's weird," Giselle said before he even got the door closed.

Frown lines creased his forehead. "When we stopped one-eightying, my first thought was we were lucky to be upright and unhurt. I don't know how there's not even a mark on your door."

A tingling rippled through her body and the hairs on the nape of her neck stood at attention. There was only one explanation as far as she was concerned. "Do you believe in magic now?"

"I'd mark it as luck," Sam said. She wasn't going to argue the point but…. "I guess we keep going since there doesn't appear to be any reason not to," he continued. "You want me to drive?"

"No. I'm fine…" Her voice petered out as an eighteen-wheeler rumbled past and she realized they could've been sitting squarely in the path of an equally big, equally lethal truck when they stopped spinning. Six feet to the left and they'd have been....

She wasn't fine. The aftermath of being behind the wheel while the vehicle spun in circles—it could have been one or twenty, she had no clue—set in and her hands began to shake so hard she couldn't steady them. Sometimes owning the power was all in knowing when to hand it over. "No. I'm not fine, and yes, I think I'd like you to drive."

Sam closed the gap between them and slipped a comforting arm around her shoulders and squeezed. His enveloping scent and touch set off an altogether different kind of trembling inside her. "No problem," he said. His warm breath stirred her hair against her temple, and the thought flitted through her mind that she'd be content to stay there forever. "It shook me up and I wasn't the one driving at the time." For one mesmerizing moment she thought he dipped his head, that his eyes flickered with an intent to kiss her, and then it was gone. He withdrew his arm and she immediately missed his touch, his warmth. "You slide over. I'll go around." He had his door open before he finished the sentence.

He got out once again and Giselle sat statue-still, momentarily frozen with disappointment over a kiss that didn't come from a man she had no business wanting it from anyway. Pulling herself together, she clambered on unsteady legs over the console and gearshift to the passenger seat. She settled back in the seat, the upholstery still warm from his body heat. The thought danced through her head that it was a bit like having him hug her from behind. Her hands shook slightly as she clicked her seat belt into place.

Sam adjusted the seat and mirrors, U-turned and they were once again on their way.

"Tell me about Barry."

His directive caught her unawares. "What?" She shook her head to clear it. "I must be more rattled than I thought. I could swear you just asked me about my ex-husband."

He smiled without looking at her, his attention firmly fixed on the highway. Some people smiled and it was a mere quirk of their lips. Sam's smile engaged his entire face, plowing lines in his cheeks and crinkling the corners of his eyes. "I did."

"But—"

"We could've both just died and I wouldn't have known a thing about your ex-husband." In profile, his nose was Romanesque. It suited his strong chin and the rest of his lived-in face.

"But why would you even care? You'd have died not knowing a whole lot of things." She would have departed this material world never knowing the taste of his mouth or the feel of his touch, other than a platonic hug or the measure of comfort he'd just doled out. She'd yearned for both even though he was forbidden territory.

"I only met him at your wedding. I'm curious as to what kind of guy you married. Indulge me." *Indulge me.* Erotically evocative. He glanced at her. "Please."

Indulge me. Please. Just how dangerous would he be if he knew how difficult it was for her to turn down *any request* for *anything* when he uttered those three words?

She shifted to look out the window away from him. She should tell him to mind his own business, but in the big scheme of things what did it matter? And nearly being killed on a highway had a way of prioritizing things. "What do you want to know?"

"How'd you meet?"

"His accounting firm was auditing one of the companies in my building. We kept bumping into one another in the ground floor coffee shop in the mornings. He always ordered a plain black and I always ordered the flavor of the week." She laughed somewhat self-consciously at having been so stupid not to see how wrong they were for one another from the beginning. "That should have told me something right away, shouldn't it?" A squat block building sat atop a brown knoll off the highway, Chuckwagon Barbecue lettered across the front in tired red paint.

"I can't imagine why it didn't send you running and screaming in the other direction," he said, coaxing a laugh from her with his droll sense of humor.

"So, there you have it. That's Barry. No cream. No sugar. No spice. End of story. End of marriage."

"I can see you're going to make me work for this." He sighed, pretending exasperation.

Okay, she was pathetically flattered he was interested in what kind of man she'd been married to.

"Basically a nice guy with a good job and a black coffee habit," he guessed.

"Essentially." She realized now that she'd thought she could distract herself with and hide behind her marriage to Barry. In short and in retrospect, she'd thought Barry would cure her of Sam-itis. It hadn't happened.

"You fell in love and got married…" he prompted.

She'd had myriad reasons. None of them the right one.

Why not just say it? She never had before. Ever. Not to her mother, Helene, her friend Margee, whom she occasionally met for dinner and drinks when their schedules allowed, or even Darren. In the distance, a hawk glided on outspread wings, diligently searching for its next meal.

"It wasn't so much love," she said slowly, letting the words find their own pace. Buried truth didn't always rush to the forefront. "He was the first guy I ever took home to meet the family who wasn't instantly panting after Helene. He didn't settle for me because he knew he didn't stand a chance with her. For the first time in my life, I wasn't playing second fiddle."

She leaned her head back against the seat. God, it felt good to say that. The accident must've left her more shaken than she'd realized to spew that out to Sam, of all people.

"Ah, a breath of refreshing honesty. At the heart of the matter, no pun intended, is the reality that people so seldom marry truly for love."

Did that mean he hadn't loved Helene? She wasn't so sure she wanted the answer and the window of opportunity to find out closed as he pressed on.

"You've obviously known some stupid bastards in your life, but Barry was a novelty and you married him." His voice lowered, softened to a verbal caress. "You were breathtakingly beautiful that day."

Breathtakingly beautiful? Her heart beat against her chest like a caged bird seeking release. No one had ever referred to her, plain-Jane Giselle, as beautiful, breathtaking or otherwise. "Are you sure you've got the right wedding and the right bride?" she said with a slightly breathless laugh.

"You were the most beautiful bride I've ever seen." There was no underscore of amusement, no self-assured grin. Instead he drove, his hands gripping the wheel, stripped of banality. "Bar none."

Blood rushed to her head. Her heartbeat seemed to echo in her ears. They both knew exactly what he'd just said. He'd been married to Helene at the time. She'd been *his* bride just four short months before Giselle's wedding. Guilt threatened to stem the sweet joy inside her that Sam McKendrick thought her the most beautiful bride. She pushed aside the guilt. Was it so wrong to embrace this one thing just this once? And what was she really taking from Helene if her sister never knew about Sam's comment?

"Thank you," she said.

"You're welcome," Sam said, watching the road.

She'd never repeat it. Ever. She didn't need to. She'd forever know, and that sweet, illicit knowledge was enough.

"It was a nice wedding," he added.

The wedding was nice. However, every other thing about marrying Barry had been a mistake. "The wedding turned out to be the only thing we agreed on. We ultimately divorced over the dry cleaning." She offered a rueful laugh. "I considered dropping off and picking up his laundry as a courtesy on my part. He saw it as my domestic duty."

Sam nodded solemnly. "Dry cleaning's a bitch. It'll kill a marriage every time."

He was so…Sam. She had the craziest notion that he understood in a way no one else had. Her parents hadn't understood at all. There'd been an unspoken censure at her decision to leave Barry, culminating in her mother's suggestion she try harder to work things out. Granted, Helene had dealt with infidelity in the dissolution of her marriage, but it really wouldn't have mattered if it had been something else.

Giselle knew her parents loved both of them, but as the oldest, Giselle had always been held to a higher standard. As the baby of the family, Helene was indulged, protected, and allowed to slide by so many things that earned Giselle the "you should've known better" reprimand.

Nope. Her parents wanted her to be happy so they'd supported her decision, but they'd never understood it. Rather than seeing a man who would spend the next twenty years trying to mold Giselle into someone she wasn't, they simply saw a pleasant enough guy with a good job and a decent income.

"The sex must've been lousy."

That jolted her out of her wool-gathering. "What?"

Sam grinned. "Good sex can usually be a Band-Aid for a marriage for at least two years."

Was he speaking from experience or simply general observation of friends? Either way, he'd nailed it. If the sex had been great, or even a little better, she could've probably tried a little longer with the dry cleaning. Barry wasn't as interested in sex as she was. She'd mistaken his rigidity for shyness. She'd thought once they were married he'd loosen up a little. Nope. No oral, and missionary position only. Nice girls didn't do *those* things. Unfortunately for them as a couple, *those* things turned her on. The best sex she'd had with Barry was when she closed her eyes and pretended he was Sam— not a good thing for her and Barry as a couple, considering they hadn't been married that long.

Things wouldn't be that way with her and Sam. She knew it. She'd known it from the beginning. Even now, she wasn't touching him but her body fairly hummed with an awareness. She seemed to instinctively respond to him. God knows, it wasn't something she chose to do, because if there was a choice, she wouldn't. But as she knew all too well, simply the *thought* of Sam did it for her when he showed up in her loosely scripted fantasies.

And this was a dangerous conversational track.

"I'm not going to discuss my sex life with you." Could she possibly sound any more prudish? Good. With the wayward direction of her thoughts and this conversation, she needed a stiff reminder—oh, poor choice of words—

of who he was and who she was and why this all needed
to stop right now. She pressed her knees together for
good measure.

He shrugged and glanced away from the road to grin,
stealing her breath with that flash of teeth and sparkling
blue eyes. She pressed her knees harder. "I wasn't asking
you to. It wasn't a leading statement. In case you haven't
noticed, if I want to know something, I ask. In this
instance, I don't need to ask. If your husband had been
better in bed, his dry cleaning wouldn't have been an
issue."

"What?" She was equally exasperated and amused
by his outlandish reasoning. "You're crazy."

"Am I?"

"Maybe if *I*'d been better in bed, his dry cleaning
wouldn't have been an issue." No. She was definitely
the crazy one to toss that particular insecurity into the
conversation.

"*You* weren't the problem," he said. His voice held
a low, caressing note. Like a finely tuned instrument,
she quivered in response. God help her if he actually
stroked one of his blunt-tipped fingers along her arm,
to her shoulder and down. Dampness gathered between
her thighs simply at the thought of his fingers on her
breast, toying with her nipple.

"How do you know?" Did he know that he'd just
turned her on, made her wet with one short sentence?
Four simple words and her body ached, hot and tight, for
him.

"Just call it intuition," he said.

He knew. It was in his eyes, in the sexy cadence of his voice. Her glance dropped to his crotch. And now *she* knew she affected him the same way he affected her.

This was why discussing sex with Sam was a bad idea. She wet her upper lip with the tip of her tongue. Sam wouldn't stop her if she unzipped his jeans, freed him and made love to his cock with her mouth while he drove down the highway. And that was exactly what she wanted to do.

She dragged her gaze away from his crotch…and found him watching her with a hungry, knowing look in his hooded eyes. A slow, wicked smile curved his mouth as he turned his attention back to the road.

They both wanted the same thing. And neither of them was getting it.

"I'm a better interviewer than you thought," he said, flashing a pleased smile that set her pulse hammering.

"Not from my perspective."

"Sure I am. I just discovered your ex-husband was lousy in bed. I said you weren't the problem, and if there hadn't been a problem, you'd have said so. Instead you asked me how I knew it wasn't you."

He'd talked circles around her. She'd have to watch herself with him, especially if they survived any other near-death experiences. Sam was dangerous. She wanted things she shouldn't want when she was around him—namely him.

Even now, even though it was a betrayal of her sister and a betrayal of her resolution to get over him, she wanted him. Not a gentle, quiet wouldn't-it-be-nice need, but a raw, every-part-of-her-craved-him craving. Another few minutes of conversation along these lines and she'd be reaching for him because her normal rationale seemed to take a hike when it came to Sam. However, she still possessed enough brain cells to know this conversation needed to end.

"Consider yourself indulged. I'm not answering any more questions."

"But you haven't totally *satisfied* my curiosity."

Satisfying Sam—her lips, her tongue, the warm, wet recesses of her mouth, her hand, all on his cock… Yet another dangerous conversational trail.

"Your satisfaction, or lack thereof, isn't my concern."

"Fantastic." Sam kept one eye on the road and the other on the massive red rocks in the distance. He itched to grab his camera. Actually, he had an even stronger itch to grab Giselle. Sequestered in the SUV with her was slowly driving him mad. He was beyond pathetic because even the sound of her breathing in the seat next to him struck him as sexy because he had a pretty good idea exactly what she'd been thinking earlier. And he'd known the precise moment she'd pulled back. It was like standing on a scorching sidewalk in the middle of summer and looking at a melting Popsicle just out of reach.

"It's humbling and inspiring," Giselle said, reverence marking her tone.

Vivid brushstrokes of blue sky, white clouds and sun glinting off the red rock gave the landscape a vibrancy at odds with the angular jutting monoliths, small, scrubby trees and brown ground. The two-lane road they were on wound through the village of Oak Creek and past an unpaved parking lot that led to hiking trails. The closer they got to Sedona, the more art galleries, restaurants, resort complexes and houses they passed, but the red rocks remained the commanding feature. They were simply incredible.

At the bottom of a hill, Sam made a hard left turn, driving over the bridge spanning Oak Creek.

"Straight ahead, back there, that was Schnebly Hill," he said. "Sedona was named for Sedona Schnebly."

"Really?" She shot him a cheeky look. "I often hare off on assignments without fully researching a location so I had no idea."

He grinned, unfazed by her smartass rejoinder. That was one of the things he liked about her.

"Lucky for you I'm here, then." Lucky for him, too, because she might be fighting it for all she was worth, but she couldn't possibly deny that there was something hot and potent between them.

"Lucky wasn't exactly what came to mind," she retorted, but there was no real sting behind the words.

They passed a stucco-walled area housing artisan shops in the style of a Mexican village, fully decked out in Christmas lights and a banner proclaiming it to be home to the Red Rock Fantasy. He'd bet his right arm she knew all about Tlaquepaque, as well.

He hung a right at the traffic light.

"Turn right in two hundred feet," the computerized female voice intoned from the dashboard GPS.

Half an hour later, the bellhop carried their bags into their home away from home for the next four days.

Sam liked what he'd seen so far. The accommodations appeared top-notch. The resort abutted the tree-lined Oak Creek and offered fantastic red rock views. They'd checked in at the elegant lodge and Giselle's eyes had widened like an excited child's at the sight of what must have been a thirty-foot Christmas tree in the lobby. A stone terrace offered creekside dining alfresco.

Rather than the lodge, they were booked into one of the cottages, which all boasted covered porches and stone chimneys. Flagstone paths meandered along the creek's edge and led through a split-rail fence and an expanse of green manicured lawn to each cottage.

Their particular bungalow overlooked the stream burbling over the stony creek bed. A fresh evergreen wreath with blue-green berries adorned the cottage door.

"Would you like the bags in the bedrooms?" the bellhop offered.

"No need, thanks," Giselle said and handed him a tip.

"We'll get it from here," Sam said simultaneously. He also pressed a couple of bucks into the young man's hand.

"Thank you." The bellhop nodded, backing toward the door. "Please let us know if there's anything we can do for you." He closed the door behind him, blocking the crisp chill of the outside.

And it suddenly seemed very, very warm in the room. Downright hot. Or maybe it was just him, because while the SUV had seemed like close confines, this was… intimate. And private.

The attraction between them two years ago hadn't gone away. It'd simply been shelved and now it was back and more potent than ever. This time, he wasn't married to her sister. There were two bedrooms within sprinting distance and a couch even closer. Unfortunately, a mountain of history remained between them that he had yet to scale. But they were definitely making headway.

Giselle stood on the other side of the luggage, her hands thrust in the pockets of her down vest, her sunglasses perched atop her head, her cheeks rosy from the December cold. His gaze snared hers and he knew a moment of triumph when he recognized the flicker of desire in her hazel eyes. She hastily averted her eyes. She could say whatever the hell she wanted to say, but he knew what he'd just seen.

"Nice place, huh?" she said, breaking the silence, interjecting a forced note of nonchalance.

He took stock of the cottage. Butter-yellow stucco walls and a leather sofa with matching armchair and ottoman arranged in front of the fireplace made for an intimate, cozy setting even though it was a sizable room. Windows overlooking the front porch flanked the fireplace and afforded a creek view. A flat-screen television occupied the far corner and an elegantly turned round table with two chairs sat in front of the window between the door and fireplace. A large rug, patterned in rich burgundy, gold, and greens on a black background, covered most of the polished hardwood floor. It was an interesting mix of French country meets Southwestern, and it worked in an elegant, sophisticated way.

The bathroom was located at the back of the cottage between two bedrooms that led off either side of the den.

"Very nice. It beats the heck out of a Motel 6," he said. "Have you stayed here before?"

"No. This is my first trip to Sedona and Monica always handles the travel arrangements." She wore the same delighted expression she'd had at the lodge when they'd checked in and Sam knew a different type of yearning that had nothing to do with sex. He wanted to be the one who put that look on her face.

A faint woodsy aroma he couldn't quite place permeated the air. "What's that smell?"

Giselle sniffed and crossed to the fireplace. She knelt on the hearth and leaned in, inhaling. He absolutely loved the shape of her ass, had from the moment she'd been in sweats and a T-shirt rooting around in that cabinet, and when she was down on her hands and knees like that…he shifted from one foot to the other.

She nodded and stood, brushing her hands together. "Juniper." What? Oh, yeah. The scent. Her cutely rounded ass was quite the distraction. "They use it for firewood."

She checked her watch and crossed back to where

the luggage sat by the front door. "I'm going to unpack and check my e-mail."

"Need any help with your suitcase?" he asked, suddenly reluctant to see her disappear behind a closed door. Although he wasn't sure walking into her bedroom with her was such a great idea, because once there, he wouldn't want to leave.

She tucked her hair behind her ear in a fidgety gesture and he could swear she'd followed his train of thought to her bedroom and subsequently her bed. "I can manage, thanks. We'll head out in about an hour."

"That's fine." He grabbed his suitcase handle. "Right or left bedroom? Your choice." Who said he couldn't be thoughtful?

"Definitely the left." She gripped her luggage pull. "It's the feng shui area of prosperity and family."

"First magic, now feng shui." Sam chuckled.

Giselle arched a condescending eyebrow as she crossed to the bedroom door, the seat of her jeans snug on her rounded bottom. "Go ahead and laugh. We'll see who's amused when we leave."

He shouldn't give her the satisfaction of asking, when she was so obviously baiting him, but what the hell, he'd bite. "Just so I know what I'm getting myself into, what's the right bedroom? What area is that?"

She paused and turned in her bedroom doorway. "Relationships, love, creativity and children. I'm here to prosper." She shot him a smug look. "I guess you're here to fall in love and procreate." She closed the door with a sharp click.

Well, who knew? Seemed as if they were finally getting on the same track. Yet one more reason to get her into his bedroom in the next three days.

5

GISELLE NEARLY laughed. The look on Sam's face when she'd dropped the feng shui bomb had almost been worth having him along. *Almost* being the definitive word.

She'd scoped out the cottage layout via the Internet site and had planned to stay in the love and relationships quadrant on the right. She wasn't sure she bought into the whole feng shui concept, but desperate women turned to desperate measures. She'd embrace feng shui, vortex magic, crystal energy…whatever, to get over that man in the other room and move on with things. Desperate times called for desperate measures. She could use some natural forces working on her behalf in the be-still-my-beating-heart area. That had been her plan when the oh-so-safe Darren was her travel partner.

Sleeping in the love relationship bedroom with Sam nearby bordered on insane, and while she might be slowly getting there, she wasn't bonafide crazy yet. And speaking of crazy, there was no way in heaven she was showing up at that vortex with him on the third day past the winter solstice without running some interference. She'd come here to get over him, not fall into a Sam McKendrick quagmire for the rest of her life.

Gooseflesh chased across her skin. The closed bedroom door should have shut him out. It hadn't. Sam's presence seemed to permeate the cottage. Unless she could get herself together and ignore him, this was going to be a long three days…and nights. And not in a good way.

She turned her back on the door and tried to block all thoughts of Sam and the energy he stirred in her, mentally settling herself into the space. She slipped off her shoes and curled her toes into the thick rug that covered most of the room. Ah. It felt great to have her shoes off.

She shrugged out of her vest and tossed it to the foot of the bed, arching her back in a stretch. She totally loved this cottage. From the ornately carved headboard and footboard to the overstuffed armchair and ottoman next to the window, she was enchanted. It was cozy without being crowded, elegant without fuss. In a word—perfect.

She pulled out her laptop and set it up on the ottoman. While it booted up, she unpacked her bags. She hated living out of a suitcase.

Content, she settled into the chair's plump cushions. She was halfway through an editorial schedule update for the next quarter—they operated on much shorter timeframes than most periodicals since they dealt with trends—when her cellphone played "We are Family," the late-Seventies tune by Sister Sledge. Helene's ringtone.

She started, glancing at the bedroom door guiltily. What was wrong with her? She hadn't done anything wrong. It wasn't as if she'd invited Sam to come along. She didn't even want him here. She didn't. She wished he was anywhere on the planet other than in the next room. She considered letting the call go to voice mail, but better to talk to Helene when she was alone than when Sam was around.

She answered and cut straight to the chase. "Hey, what's going on?"

"I was out doing some last-minute Christmas shopping," Helene said, "and I stopped by and checked on the bench. It's beautiful."

"Good. I think they're going to love it." After their father's retirement, he'd devoted himself to becoming a master gardener and recruited their mom as his assistant. Their green-thumb parents were slowly but surely transforming a nice enough backyard into a spectacular garden showcase. She and Helene had gone together and custom-ordered a garden bench for their parents' Christmas gift. Actually, it had been Giselle's idea and she'd been the one to find the artist and commission the bench. Helene might've taken last year with the post-Christmas cruise, but this year the Christmas-gift points squarely belonged to Giselle.

It had all started when the girls were still young and their parents were funding the gift giving. The girls had been encouraged to go together to select one gift for both parents. A heck of a lot easier on the Christmas budget than two kids buying separate presents for two parents. It had become something of a competition between Giselle and Helene to see who could come up with the best gift idea for the parents each Christmas. Sort of the same way everything was a friendly competition between them. Giselle wasn't the least surprised that Helene had been by to check on the gift so she'd at least have some input.

"I wish you were going to be here when they deliver it," Helene said petulantly.

Giselle pushed out of the chair. The latest delivery available was midday Christmas Eve. "I'll be there late Christmas Eve."

"I don't understand why you had to plan this trip at Christmas."

Giselle pulled back the curtain and the sheers. Wow, nice red rock view. She laughed. "Mostly because the winter solstice is a naturally occurring event and nature doesn't really do the change-up to accommodate holiday schedules." It wasn't as if they hadn't covered this ground before—several times, in fact. Helene understood exactly *why* but she didn't like it. That was the problem: Helene wasn't getting her way. And well, maybe she didn't get the exact why of it.

Yes, Giselle felt guilty she was the one screwing up a long-standing family tradition. They always gathered at her parents' home early on Christmas Eve. But dammit, this was important to her, although she hadn't told her family just why or how important.

"Anyway," Giselle said, "you've got some selective memory going there. Have you forgotten the year you eloped and didn't show up until midday on Christmas?"

"Oh, Giselle, that was different. I'd just gotten married." Giselle could almost see her sister waving a dismissive hand. "Not that *that* wasn't a mistake. But anyway, you're there now. What do you think so far?" Helene didn't understand the appeal of Sedona, especially when it threw a spanner into the family tradition. But while she might be irritated by the trip, she was still been interested.

"It's stunning." *And by the way, you won't believe how weird things have turned out. I'm here with Sam. Right, your ex-husband. No kidding. He's in the other bedroom.*

"That's good. Is the cottage as nice as it looked online?" Giselle had sent her a link to the resort.

"Better, actually."

"Leave it to my older sister." A teasing note crept into Helene's voice.

Giselle preferred her sister's teasing over sulking any day. She smiled. "What?"

"You're in a place voted one of the most beautiful in this country and you're sharing a romantic cottage with Darren." *Correction. I'm sharing with your philandering ex-husband who still gets under my skin.* "It's just wrong, Giselle." Amusement tinged Helene's voice. If she only knew the utter irony.

Tell her. Tell her now. Giselle should just laugh and toss it into the conversation. Except Helene was talking about being in Sedona romantically, and dropping Sam into that equation struck Giselle as supremely bad timing. And she'd admit it, she got to put off something unpleasant for a little longer. Why face today what she could put off until later this week?

Afterward. She'd tell Helene and the folks afterward, when it was history. They'd all gather in the kitchen to put away leftovers and clean the Christmas dinner dishes and she'd laugh and relay how awkward it had been. *That* struck her as a much better plan. And she'd lay the foundation now that regardless of whom she was here with, it was in a professional capacity.

"It's a business trip," Giselle said.

"There's nothing wrong with mixing a little business with pleasure sometimes. It's not as if you're in a strict corporate setting. You could be having a romantic interlude."

Her sister so wouldn't be saying that if she had even an inkling who was in the other room. "Moot point."

Helene's laughter trilled on the other end. "Okay, okay. Strictly business. Are you bringing anyone for Christmas?"

They both knew the question was rhetorical. "No. I'm coming alone." Even the year she and Barry had been married, he'd gone to his parents' solo and she to hers.

"Okay. Call me in a few days and let me know how it's going. I want to hear all about it when you get back."

They ended the call and Giselle breathed a sigh of relief that Sam hadn't knocked on her door with some question. *That* would have made for an awkward phone call with Helene. She was fairly certain her sister would still recognize Sam's voice.

She leaned her head against the cool windowpane. She'd recognize Sam's voice. And his scent. And the way every nerve ending in her body fired into awareness when he was near.

She pushed away from the window and straightened her shoulders. Dropping back into the chair, she checked her e-mail, determined to put Sam out of her mind. She dealt with the more pressing issues in her in-box and signed off.

She closed her eyes, inhaling through her nose, pulling in the air all the way to her abdomen and slowly exhaling, releasing the tension. Maybe that's why she couldn't shut Sam out. They'd lapsed into personal conversation, and personal conversation with Sam left her sexually and emotionally tense. No more talking about anything except Sedona and the article. She would treat Sam with distant, professional courtesy, as if he were a stranger. Except the article was all about attraction and falling in love. Okay. Equally bad idea.

She only had to get through the next three days. No more discussions about her ex-husband and marriage and satisfying anything or anyone. And no more lapsing into sexual fantasies. Just because she had an active imagination and being around Sam had her constantly thinking about sex didn't mean anything other than… well, that he made her horny and she thought about having sex with him…a lot.

But he didn't know that. She'd given herself away

today in the car, staring at his crotch. No more. She'd put on her poker face and ignore the sizzle between them.

From here on, it was strictly business.

SAM CAPPED the lens on his camera, satisfied with the photos he'd taken so far, and followed Giselle as she turned into the side street that ran perpendicular to their route. They'd walked from the cottage through Sedona's main street, Highway 89A, lined with art galleries and an array of small shops offering a little bit of everything, from the usual tourist fare of cheap T-shirts to high-end home furnishings. Every direction offered a spectacular view of bright blue skies, wispy clouds and towering red rocks. There was definitely something different about this place. It was as if he were somehow more closely connected to the earth and sky. He could see how people might convince themselves special things could happen here.

The afternoon was crisp, but not cold, the air fresh and clean. Giselle had been surprisingly patient with him taking so many photos. He'd included her in several of the shots.

A shingled sign hung over a wood-and-glass door, the wood portion painted a deep purple. The lettering on the glass advertised that Good Vibrations offered aura readings and spiritual recovery sessions. What the hell was a spiritual recovery?

"This is where you're hooking up with Glinda the Good Witch?" he said. He appreciated the beauty of the place, but he was a skeptic when it came to all the attendant hocus-pocus mumbo jumbo.

"White Dove is actually a vortex shaman," Giselle said, looking down her freckled nose at him, which was more cute than haughty. "Feel free to wait outside if you're nervous about meeting her."

White Dove was the woman who purportedly understood the metaphysical and spiritual implications behind the vortex phenomena immediately following the winter solstice. In other words, she was behind the come-fall-in-love angle.

"Oh no. I wouldn't miss this."

Sam followed Giselle's nicely rounded backside into the store. A bell mounted over the door tinkled, heralding their arrival. The haunting, soothing melody of an Indian flute and the scent of incense floated on the air. At first glance, crystals of varying shapes and sizes seemed to hover above them, but on closer inspection they hung suspended from the ceiling by thin lines—maybe fishing line.

Something inexplicable seemed to pass through him, surround him. He wasn't altogether sure he liked this shop.

"Welcome." A woman's voice hailed them from behind a curtained doorway at the back of the long, narrow shop. She emerged, tall and thin, of indeterminate age, a silvery blond plait hanging down her back. Sam knew he sometimes wasn't the most sensitive guy, but even he recognized the sense of peace that radiated from her. "I'm White Dove."

He'd expected long flowing robes and maybe a feathered headdress. Instead, she wore jeans and a collared blue shirt. A simple crystal necklace hung from a delicate chain about her neck.

Giselle introduced herself and Sam, and she and White Dove hugged like old friends. Within a minute, the two women stood at the back of the store, engrossed in reviewing materials and details. Sam wandered about and found himself drawn to a gemology display in a case near the front window.

"Interesting, isn't it?"

He startled. He hadn't heard the other woman approach. Hell, he'd thought he, Giselle and White Dove were the only ones here. He recovered his aplomb. The shop definitely had him on edge.

"Um, yeah."

"I'm Lisle Gilbreath," she said. She bore a remarkable resemblance to the picture of the Virgin Mary that had hung in his mother's den. Brown hair framed her oval face in soft waves. A momentary melancholy embraced him at the memory of his mother. Even though Ms. Gilbreath's face was serene and unlined, Sam guessed she was in her late forties or early fifties. "Peace be with you today."

"Peace be with you also," he intoned, an automatic response prompted by years of mother-enforced Mass attendance.

"Hold out your hand." Her soft voice whispered through him like the wind sighing through the trees.

The back of his neck prickled and for an instant he

considered refusing, but what was the harm in doing as she asked? It seemed an innocuous enough request. He offered her his palm. She plucked a smooth, egg-shaped pink stone from the velvet-lined display case and placed it in his hand. A faint vibration emanated from the stone to his palm.

"Rose quartz." She smiled at his momentary surprise. "Each stone, each gem carries an energy, a vibration with it."

"Okay." He nodded even though he was pretty damn sure it was nothing more than a parlor trick. But he wanted to see just how far she'd go with this. What was her angle? Would she try to talk him into buying an expensive vibrational frequency stone? "Interesting."

He returned the stone to her. From across the store Giselle gestured with her hands while she spoke to White Dove. Giselle's movements struck him as sensually elegant.

"A man doesn't necessarily have to seek clarity in order to find it," the woman said, snagging his attention.

"I beg your pardon."

"Clarity."

"Clarity of what?"

She smiled. "Of whatever you need at that point in time."

"And what if I don't need clarity?" he asked, playing devil's advocate.

"Then you are a lucky and most unusual person indeed."

"Let's say I do. What if I need clarity on a whole bunch of things?"

"Then the strongest need is addressed first."

"The squeaky wheel theory?"

"I suppose you could call it that." She tilted her head to one side and smiled. "The wind, the lack of damage to your vehicle today… None of that was happenstance."

What the hell? "How'd you know about that?" He nodded. "You must've heard Giselle talking to White Dove."

"No. She's mentioned nothing."

"But I don't believe—"

She laughed, and it reminded him of the tinkling bell above the door. "It doesn't matter whether you believe. This isn't the Polar Express." He must've looked as if he didn't know what the hell she was talking about. "You know, the children's book made into a movie." She waved a hand in dismissal and offered another smile. "Never mind." The same inexplicable sensation he'd experienced when he walked into the shop slid over him again. "I've been saving something for you, Sam."

She opened a drawer in the counter, reached into the far recesses and withdrew a velvet draw-string pouch. *Sam.* She'd called him Sam yet he hadn't introduced himself to her.

She withdrew a necklace. It was actually a carved stone disc on a leather cord.

He shook his head. "I don't do jewelry." He'd only

ever worn a wedding ring for the brief time he'd been married. He wasn't a necklace or bracelet kind of guy.

She reached up and fastened the leather strip around his neck as if he hadn't spoken.

"Hey, I said—"

The amulet settled against his skin, in the V of his shirt, and a jolt speared through him. The stone glowed warm against him, that same warmth spreading through him. And as if he'd plunged headfirst into a heated pool, he found himself buoyed by a sexuality, a carnal need not his own. He wasn't sure how he knew it wasn't his, but the certainty settled within him.

"Wait…what's happening? This isn't my—"

"Sometimes our own clarity is mirrored through or found through another."

It was as if a part of his mind were looking at something through an unfocused, filtered lens on a screen in part of his head. His cock felt heavy between his legs. "What the…"

"Clarity often comes with true sexual fulfillment. This stone allows you to glimpse, to tune in to the fantasies of your lover. But you must never abuse this. It can't become a tool of power. It can only be used for fulfilling her needs and to bring her pleasure."

That didn't make any sense. "But if it's for my clarity, wouldn't it be my fantasies?"

"No. True pleasure is found in giving and it is in giving that we find fulfillment."

"I don't have a lover right now." So he felt a little odd having the necklace on, but come on, having the inside track to a woman's fantasies... "So does this mean I'll know the fantasy of any woman I date? Any woman I sleep with? Any woman I pass on the street? Any woman I want to read?" Giselle?

He didn't believe a bit of it, but it was a kick-ass story. If it was so powerful why didn't he know *her* fantasy?

"Because *I* haven't awakened your inner desire."

Once again, she'd ignored his spoken questions and answered the one he'd posed in his head. It was a little creepy the way she did that, but she must have just been hazarding a lucky guess. Anyone with a lick of sense would question all of this.

He ran his finger over the stone's smooth surface and a slight tingle shot through him. "How do I turn the fantasy detector off?"

"That's easy enough." That tinkling laughter again. "You take it off."

Time to lead her to the close. "And how much does this cost?"

"Who can put a price on clarity, on fulfilling passion?" She paused and he steeled himself. She was doing a great job of building up its value. "Consider it a gift."

He faltered for a second, taken aback. "You're just giving it to me? For free?" She'd picked the wrong guy because he'd known from the time he was a kid that nothing came free. Not everything could be bought, but everything came with a price.

"You're absolutely right that nothing's free and

everything comes with a price, Sam. But that's what you need to figure out—the price of clarity. You'll know when you do."

Ah. She was taking a make-me-an-offer tactic—

"No," she said, interrupting this thought. "The price you pay is from yourself, to yourself."

Dammit. Would she stop answering questions he hadn't asked aloud? And all of that aside, her *giving* it to him just sealed the deal that it was a bunch of mumbo jumbo, because pretty much every guy he knew would pay big bucks to tap into his woman's fantasies. "Really, you should give it to someone who believes in this type of stuff. It's just wasted on me."

"But it spoke to me and it now belongs to you," she said. Sam blinked, several times for good measure. He didn't care if he looked goofy. Maybe she was pulling some crazy hypnotic stuff with him. "When you're through with it, you'll know when it's time to give it to someone else."

"You don't want it back?"

"It belongs to you now. I wouldn't recommend it, but you could even sell it on eBay if that's what you decide you should do with it. There is one tricky part. You won't know whether it's really you in her fantasy or if you're simply superimposing yourself on her fantasy."

Ah, he had her now. "But I thought the whole point was to bring clarity, and that just muddies the water."

"It's the natural progression. Dark precedes light as obscurity precedes clarity."

He opened his mouth to ask— Whatever it was flew

out of his head because at that moment Giselle looked at him from across the room. Her gaze tangled with his, and it was as if the small screen in his head suddenly came into sharp, precise focus.

Excitement ricocheted through him, pinging off the desire that swept through him. Giselle. Was he really in her head?

In his mind's eye, he watched the scene play out on the screen. *He scanned a crowded room filled with beautiful women and Giselle. Of all the women, Giselle stood out as exotic amid such unrelenting loveliness. He stood on the periphery and he knew he could pick any woman he wanted. And still it was Giselle who captured his attention, his imagination, his desire.* Even as he stood in the crystal shop, his blood pooled between his thighs and lust thickened his cock. He braced his legs apart to accommodate his hard-on.

He pointed at Giselle. He shouldered his way through the other women to stand at her side, fixated only on her, throbbing for her. He didn't know what he said to her. It didn't come through in his head. Nor did he know her reply. *She lifted her chin, and the sensuality in her gaze tightened his balls in very real time in the middle of the shop.* And then like the end of a silent movie reel, the fantasy screen in his mind faded to black and then to nothingness.

What the hell had just happened? None of it had been controlled by him.

In the scene that had just played out in his head, what had he said to Giselle? What was her reply? He sensed on a gut level that he'd never know what that particular conversation was about if he took off the amulet. He slowly lowered his hands to his sides.

If that was a sexual fantasy…well, they'd both been fully clothed and there'd been no touching, which made the unknown conversation all the more important.

With a start, he realized, weirder still, that Lisle Gilbreath was gone. He looked around but didn't see her anywhere in the shop. Any questions he wanted answered he'd have to answer on his own.

If this was real, if he'd just seen inside Giselle's head, he was about to discover all her secret fantasies. And he was going to do his damndest to fulfill every one of them.

Whether she wanted one or not, Giselle had just found herself a love slave.

6

"I'D RECOMMEND visiting the Airport Vortex today," White Dove said. "It's the closest and involves the least amount of hiking. You might run out of daylight otherwise."

Giselle nodded. "That's what I was thinking, too." Plus, she could use a hearty dose of Airport Vortex. According to her research notes, the energy there bolstered your internal strength in taking charge of your life. The energy there also strengthened a person's ability to figure out how to get what you wanted out of life. She needed to shore up both of those areas to deal with Sam on this trip. "I'll call late this afternoon to confirm tomorrow's and Tuesday's interviews."

White Dove nodded in approval. She'd arranged for Giselle to interview Davie and Aleana March, who had met at the vortex three days past the winter solstice thirty years ago. They were slated for a 1 p.m. interview tomorrow. Then she'd meet at three with Dan and Virginia Watson, a young couple from Pennsylvania. Both couples were here to celebrate a second honeymoon and both were dedicated to energy renewal on "Love Day," as Giselle was thinking of dubbing it,

because "three days past the winter solstice" was so
stinking awkward. The following day she would interview the remaining couples. Early Christmas Eve
morning she'd accompany all the couples, eight in total,
to the vortex for their ceremony. White Dove had been
great to work with via e-mail and even more likeable
in person.

And Giselle had tried very hard to keep her mind on
the topic at hand but that was easier said than done with
Sam here too. During her discussion with White Dove,
she'd actually found part of her mind playing out a
familiar fantasy, the one nonsexual fantasy that was ultimately sexual in nature since it set the stage for all the
others.

Good thing she was a multitasker. And it was a good
thing her fantasizing lapse had involved the lone innocuous, G-rated one from her repertoire since she suspected White Dove possessed some psychic powers.
Giselle preferred to keep her harder-faster, down-and-
dirty fantasies private.

White Dove paused and took a step back, "You have
a very powerful aura."

Giselle had debated requesting an aura reading. She
knew each person emitted energy, an aura. Some people
possessed the ability to read and interpret the energy as
colors. Once again, she wasn't so sure she bought into
it, but the possibility fascinated her. "Really? I have a
powerful aura?"

"Yes. It's very bright and strong and intensely sexual."

"That's surprising." Did frustration show up?

"Is it really?" White Dove quirked one of her silver eyebrows over her bright blue eyes. "I don't think you're surprised at all, just a little uncomfortable with acknowledging how powerful and prevalent your aura is, which is perhaps why it's dark and muddled nearest you." She nodded toward the front of the store where Sam stood thumbing through a book. The sun slanted through the window, picking out golden highlights in his dark brown hair. "You both have very strong sexual auras. It was apparent when I met the two of you, especially together."

Giselle felt a blush crawl up her neck. She didn't say anything because she didn't know how she was supposed to respond to that. Was it so very obvious how Sam affected her?

White Dove continued, "When the right two people connect, physically, mentally and emotionally, they can have a synergistic effect on one another. I believe that's the case with you two."

Giselle's heart thumped harder and faster in her chest. "But he…I…we don't…it's not like that."

"Are you so sure?"

"Look at him and then look at me." Sam inspired women to drool. Giselle inspired men to look right through her.

"I have." White Dove imbued her simple nod with wisdom. "Sedona is a place of healing and self-actualization but you have to be willing to follow your path when it appears before you, even if it's not what you anticipated. Sometimes what we think we want isn't what we need and vice versa."

Giselle had sought to bury, cauterize, ignore the fact that she wanted Sam McKendrick. She'd wanted Sedona to be a catalyst for change, a new start, a cleansing of Sam. And then like some bad karmic turn, he'd shown up on the very trip designed to scour him from topping her want list. He wasn't just topping her want list, he *was* her want list, even though she didn't want to want him, which was really complicated. "And what about when you want what you can't have?"

White Dove regarded her with knowing eyes. "Ah, but that's human nature, isn't it? To want the very thing we're forbidden to have? And then we want it all the more for that very reason."

Giselle felt as if White Dove had peered into her soul. Pretense seemed useless and counterintuitive. "He was married to my very beautiful sister." His taste didn't run to women who looked like Giselle, even if there'd been a connection between them from first glance. "And he cheated on her." And Giselle's taste didn't run to shallow men who couldn't be trusted, even if she couldn't seem to stop wanting him in a strictly physical sense.

"Is your sister still in love with him?"

Helene had recovered from her broken marriage in record time, remarrying within three months. There were times Giselle had wondered just how in love she'd ever been in the first place, but then maybe Sam's betrayal had annihilated whatever love had been there. "It doesn't really matter, does it? He's not trustworthy."

"Have you ever asked him why?" White Dove's

quiet question seemed to ride on the rising notes of the Indian flute playing in the background.

Giselle worried the zipper pull on her vest. "No. I haven't seen him in a year and a half and not since it happened. But I wouldn't have asked him regardless. It wasn't my business."

"Perhaps it is now," White Dove said. Her eyes were kind, understanding. "You can't move forward with the new until old business is resolved. And every person deserves a fair trial," she added softly.

Sam returned the book to the shelf and looked over his shoulder to where she and White Dove stood talking. Even with the store separating them, his glance unsettled her. And maybe that was precisely why he'd wound up on this trip with her. She'd wanted to howl in frustration but she now saw the situation clearly and understood. She couldn't keep running away from Sam; she had to confront him and her attraction, both literally and figuratively, before she could move on. She had to finish the business that had started two years ago. And she didn't see how she could do that without wading into the personal breach.

Giselle nodded, swallowing her trepidation.

She and White Dove started toward the front of the store, toward Sam.

"Just remember, Giselle, caution is wise," the older woman murmured, "fear is debilitating."

SAM MARVELED at the surge of energy coursing through him from his vantage point atop the flat red rock that marked the Airport Vortex. It had been a short drive from the resort to the parking lot and then a very short hike to the top of the rock.

He wasn't sure what he'd expected. Maybe a sign with an arrow that announced Vortex or a small chasm with a rainbow-hued air mass constantly swirling out of it.

Instead, he found merely a flat rock, but there was no mistaking the shift in energy around him and inside him. Actually, the vortex itself was a few feet back down the rise to the right, marked by the twisted limbs of the junipers growing there. The strong energy of the vortex affected the trees' growth, giving their branches a helical twist, most pronounced where the energy was greatest.

However, the flat top of the hill afforded the best views.

"Fantastic view, don't you think?" he said. Sedona spread before them like a 3-D model. Away from the town itself, houses were perched on the hillsides in the undercarriage of the ever-towering rocks ringing the area.

"It's beautiful," Giselle said, pushing her sunglasses to the top of her head, as if she didn't want the view filtered.

In that moment, his focus shifted and everything else became backdrop. He only saw Giselle. The sparkle in her eyes, the curve of her lips, the tease of her hair against her cheek.

"Yes, beautiful." He had an eye for beauty, for composition. He traded in the transformations wrought by a subtle lighting change or a shift in focus that turned the ordinary into the extraordinary. He wasn't sure whether it was lighting or composition or simply location, but Giselle radiated an irresistible sensuality that lit her from within.

Like iron filings in the presence of a magnet, he was drawn to her. He didn't stop to consider, debate, justify. Instead, he simply *did,* caught up in something bigger than himself.

In one step he closed the gap between them and reached for her.

"Sam, I don't think...." Her words trailed off but she didn't step away.

He bracketed her head in his hands, plying his thumbs against her soft skin, sinking his fingers into the thick richness of her hair to mold the fine bones of her scalp. "I know. Me, either."

He'd waited two years for this moment, possibly a lifetime. He wasn't rushing now.

She splayed her palms against his chest, as if to hold him at bay. Her touch scorched him through his shirt, branding him as hers. Her green-brown eyes widened at the heavy thumping of his heart beneath her hand. *You do that to me, you always have.* For a long moment, he felt the pause inside her, the hesitation, and then, rather than push him away, she curled her fingers into the edges of his jacket as if to hold on.

Sam lowered his forehead to rest against hers, absorbing her scent, her touch. Her breath gusted warm and sweet against his face on her sigh. He feathered tender kisses across her brow, over her lowered lids, her lashes tickling his lips, to the plush softness of her cheek.

"Sam." She seemed to breathe his name in an exhalation of desire, wonderment and capitulation. She slid her hands up his chest and looped her arms about his neck, her fingers stroking the nape of his neck above his collar. Her touch felt so good.

He brushed his mouth over hers, their breath mingling, the chill wind not permeating the heat between them. For a second, the universe seemed to stand still. He settled his lips on hers. She tasted faintly of mint-tinged lip balm.

And that was his last coherent thought as a torrent of want and need, held in check for so long, was unleashed and raged between them, bound them. She arched into him, opening her mouth to him, her hunger matching his own. He pulled her closer into a perfect fit against him.

Sam stroked his tongue into the sweet, hot warmth of her mouth. She slid her tongue against his, a velvet entreaty. Sweet. Hot. His.

Sam, who was always in control, felt dazed, slightly disoriented, when they finally broke apart. The chilly wind, the red-rock vista, and the woman who stepped away from him posthaste reminded him. Sedona. Airport Vortex. Ex-sister-in-law. Right.

Giselle crossed her arms over her chest. "You shouldn't have done that."

If she was looking for remorse, she wouldn't find

any from him. "If you really felt that way, then I guess you shouldn't have kissed me back."

"Maybe not. Positively not. But you started it." She planted her hands on her hips and glared at him, looking adorably disheveled from his hands in her hair and their kiss. "We're here to work together. You can't go around kissing me whenever you feel like it."

Was she aware her nipples were standing at rigid attention against her T-shirt? He was aware enough for both of them. And he felt so damn good after kissing her he wanted to shout and punch his fist in the air. He grinned instead. "Hmm. Kissing you whenever I feel like it. That particular option hadn't occurred to me but I think I like the idea."

"It's not funny, Sam."

"You know, sweetheart, I could've sworn you kissed me right back with more than a little enthusiasm. And just for the record, I don't mind a bit if you kiss me like that whenever you feel like it."

"Try never again."

"Now, *that* is disappointing."

She looked away from him. "Are you satisfied now that you've had your comparison? Now that you've seen how one of the Randolph sisters stacks up against the other?"

What the hell?

She looked at him and the accusation was there in her eyes. And did she ever have it wrong. "Helene never crossed my mind."

"I don't believe you."

"Believe it." Once again, he closed the gap between them, nearly losing his footing on the uneven ground. He caught her wrist in his hand and her pulse raced beneath his fingertips. "Sweetheart, the only way Helene could be here is if *you* brought her with you. I've wanted to do that since the first time I met you. You and I both know that kiss has been in the making since that Christmas Day." He brought her wrist to his mouth and pressed a kiss to the delicate blue veins.

"You're crazy." Color stained her cheeks and she tugged her wrist free of him. She stepped back. "It won't happen again. The end."

Ah. Sam didn't miss the fact that while she might had called him crazy, she didn't deny that she'd wanted to kiss him as well since that night.

She might proclaim their kiss the end, but he didn't need an amulet to tell him this was just the beginning.

7

GISELLE PERCHED on the restaurant bar stool and sipped the red wine, letting it sit on her tongue for a moment before she swallowed.

"What do you think?" Sam asked, his knee glancing against hers, the brief contact zinging through her. Earlier it had been his hand under her elbow as she got out of the car, then his hand against the small of her back as they crossed the room to have a drink at the bar until a table was available in the dining room. They were meaningless touches that nonetheless singed her and kept her on edge. What'd she think? She thought he was driving her mad.

But he was actually inquiring about the wine he'd recommended, an Argentinean malbec. So he remembered after two years that she preferred dry red wine. Big deal.

"It's quite good. I like it."

"I'm glad. I thought you might." He lifted his glass and tasted. "Full-bodied, complex with dark undertones."

She was in so much trouble because they were just discussing wine but his words and his voice held a seductive pull for her. Who was she kidding? Certainly not herself anymore. His simply *being* held a seductive pull for her. Her pulse quickened and moisture gathered between her thighs.

Giselle was saved from responding when he frowned and reached for his cell phone. "Excuse me, I'm vibrating." He swore under his breath. "I really need to take this call." While the sound in the restaurant bar wasn't deafening, it was noisy enough. He placed his hand over the receiver and spoke to Giselle. "I'm going to step outside so I can hear. This may take a few minutes."

"No worries. I'll finish my wine. Maybe yours, too, if you're gone long enough," she added, trying to keep it light, letting him know she was perfectly happy with him gone.

He grinned and slid off the stool. Against her better judgment, which was apparently on hiatus, she watched him cross the room. Giselle knew he'd played college football and he still moved with the athletic grace of a running back. And a touch of arrogance.

He's not for you, her ever-vigilant conscience reminded her yet again. *Doesn't 'off limits' mean anything to you? Did you forget he was married to Helene…and slept around on her?* Not likely. Except when he'd kissed her, that very thought *had* deserted her.

She sipped at her wine. Had she made the wrong choice coming out to dinner with Sam?

When they'd finished up at the Airport Vortex, without any further physical contact, they'd headed back to the cottage. She'd considered sequestering herself in her room with room service, but she refused to run and hide. Not that she had anything to prove to Sam but *she'd* know she was hiding in her room. Wasn't that her big takeaway from her visit with White Dove? No more running. No more hiding.

What did it really matter whether she was sitting in a crowded restaurant waiting for a table or cloistered in her cottage bedroom? She couldn't escape the memory, the impact of that kiss.

Over the past two years she'd fantasized about kissing Sam, and a whole helluva lot more than kissing. But it had all been conjecture. Now she *knew* his kiss, his touch, his taste. And the knowledge was devastating, titillating, maddening. How could she experience that kiss and not want more of the same? How could she not ache to be in his arms again?

Granted, she had a tendency to overthink things, but she had spent the rest of the afternoon turning that kiss over in her head. Had kissing Sam been so incredible because they were standing at the vortex? Or because she knew Sam was off limits? Or because it'd been a fairly long time since she'd kissed anyone? Or was it, as White Dove had said, because Giselle and Sam were potent together?

She had a couple of options. She could kiss Sam when she wasn't standing in front of a vortex that emitted powerful energy to see if a second kiss even came close to the first. However, wasn't that inviting trouble? Maybe Helene hadn't actually been there, but she'd certainly been tapping Giselle on the shoulder.

She could kiss another man at the vortex to see if it elicited the same spine-tingling, nipple-tightening response. The problem was finding a man other than Sam to drag up to the vortex with her.

The wisest course of action was to try to forget about it. Unfortunately, she wasn't so sure she could when four hours later her lips still resonated with the feel of his mouth against hers. She wasn't naive enough to think Sam had forgotten that kiss but she also didn't think he was sitting around still worked up over it the way she was.

She wasn't so sure that having a glass of wine was a good idea, but short of canceling the trip, nothing seemed like a good idea…and she wasn't canceling the trip.

Giselle ordered another glass of wine—she'd just been kidding Sam about drinking his—determined to put herself in the here and now instead of dwelling on Sam and Helene and that kiss and the whole stinking mess that had exploded in her face when Sam strolled into her cubicle Friday morning.

She liked the atmosphere in this place. A combination of down-home and upscale, with a blues guitarist in one corner of the bar and linen-covered tables in the dining area. And she thought it was fun the way they'd strung Christmas lights around the top of the oval bar area.

Giselle watched the people in the room. Several couples sat perched on the stools, engaged in conversation. Three women, early to mid-twenties and gorgeous, came in and sat at the bar on the opposite side of Giselle. She sized them up as flavored-martini drinkers. She grinned to herself as the bartender mixed and presented them with a Cosmo and two Green Apple tinis.

At the end of the bar, a man and woman weren't having a good time. Giselle was ninety-nine percent certain it was a blind date. The woman, not unattractive but not stunning, either, sat pleating a cocktail napkin and looking as if she'd appreciate a big black hole swallowing her. Her date, a sandy-haired guy with a receding hairline, blatantly checked out the three single women farther down the bar.

Giselle shifted uncomfortably on the bar stool, feeling the woman's discomfort. Giselle had been there and done that. She silently willed the other woman to get up and walk out rather than sit there miserably while her date checked out other women. She had to hand it to the martini trio; they weren't giving Mr. Sleazoid the time of day.

Suddenly a look passed between the three. They all sat a little straighter and smiled toward the door—the universal look of women homing in on a man. A tingle chased down her spine and Giselle knew they were looking at Sam. He must've wrapped up his phone call. She pivoted on the bar stool toward the doorway, fully expecting to see him sizing up the martini sippers.

She froze. Sam stood looking at her…and there was no mistaking the look. It snared her from across the room. Time seemed to slow. It was every gaze across a crowded room she'd ever seen in the movies or read about in a book. It claimed her.

Her heart thumped hard and fast in her chest and she wrapped her fingers around the wineglass stem as if it were a lifeline rather than fragile glass that could snap and shatter. Didn't he know that any, or all, of the three gorgeous women at the bar were his for the asking?

He either didn't know or didn't care. A slow half-smile curved his lips and lit his eyes. It proclaimed *I want you.* His gaze never wavered as he made his way to her.

Panic underscored the thrill elicited by the declaration in his hooded blue eyes. A sense of déjà vu swamped her. How many times had she fantasized this very thing? The man of her choice only having eyes for her. Except Sam wasn't really the man of her choice; he was just the forbidden temptation, wasn't he? Regardless, she couldn't look away. Her body tingling, she licked suddenly dry lips, and his eyes darkened.

Sam slid onto his stool and angled closer to her. He invaded her personal space. His leg pressed against her knee, and while the rest of him didn't touch her, mere inches separated them.

She couldn't ignore the sexuality shimmering between them. Fantasies were one thing, but reality was about to step in. Didn't she know that she couldn't trust that look? Hadn't they shared that look on the stairs, on the love seat two years ago, and hadn't he slept with another woman other than the one he was married to? Maybe availability was a deciding factor. She'd usher reality in hard and fast.

"Those three women are giving you the eye."

"What three women?"

"Across the bar. With the martinis. Two blondes and a brunette."

He didn't even glance their way. "Are they?"

She couldn't leave it alone. "You could have your pick of any of them. Probably all three. They're all quite pretty."

"Good for them."

"Aren't you even going to check them out?"

"No. I'm not interested in *them*. I don't want them."

"But how do you know…" she trailed off as he reached up and quieted her with his fingertip against her lips. Giselle quivered inside.

"Because I know exactly who I want."

GISELLE STARED at him.

He wasn't playing games or using the amulet to his advantage. It just felt damn good to say what he'd held inside for so long.

He wanted her more fiercely than he'd ever wanted a woman before—ever. He'd finished his conversation with his assistant Martha regarding a gallery showing and walked back into the restaurant, and it had hit him right between the eyes. He honestly couldn't say what the other people in the room looked like because he hadn't noticed them. It was as if he'd stepped into the fantasy that he'd seen in his head that afternoon. It was a scene previously scripted, but he wasn't playing a role. This was real and intense.

He knew exactly who he wanted. So did she. She just wasn't ready to own up to it yet.

"Sam, I think…" Giselle began, then hesitated. "Our table's ready," she said. She held up the blinking "pager" restaurants handed out to wait-listed guests like a trophy.

Within minutes they were seated at a corner table and had dispensed with ordering. The waitress left and Giselle glanced around the restaurant, looking everywhere but at him. "I wonder if the stone used in the flooring is local."

Sam smiled at her attempt to defuse the attraction pulsing between them with the mundane. He wasn't arrogant but he knew she wanted him. He'd felt her watching him when he walked out earlier. He'd also felt it in her kiss. Actions spoke so much louder than words.

He glanced across the table at her and couldn't look away. She literally stole his breath. There was a luminosity about her that gave her skin a healthy glow and put a sparkle in her eyes. She was like a succulent piece of ripe fruit.

"You look lovely tonight," he said.

"It's the dim lighting in here." She laughed self-consciously and sipped from her wine glass, as if it were a shield. "You can't see me, as well."

"Stop." Her eyes widened in surprise at his directive. "I can see you just fine. You've got a radiance about you. Maybe that short hike agreed with you earlier today." *Or maybe it was that kiss at the vortex.* He didn't say it, but then he didn't have to. The same thought was reflected in the hazel depths of her eyes.

She developed a sudden interest in the white linen table cloth. Silence stretched between them until she squared her shoulders and looked at him. "Why are you saying something like that?"

"Because it's true."

Was that a flash of anger or frustration in her eyes? She shook her head. "Let's just keep this real between us."

"I'm being as real as I know how to be."

"Well, that's the problem, isn't it? Apparently deception is second nature to you."

Oh, yeah. She was firmly seating Helene at the table with them. Was it to keep him at arm's length or to keep herself in check? Either way, his ex-wife was now here. And much as he didn't want to deal with the issue of Helene and where and how their marriage fell apart, he knew he and Giselle had to deal with it. It was the only way to move forward. "I've said it before and I'll say it again. I made a mistake."

She leaned in toward him. "Why? Why'd you sleep around on her? She's beautiful, talented, so why wasn't she enough for you?"

Giselle and Helene were close, but he was pretty damn sure Helene had only fed her the truth in dribs and drabs. Helene had presented the truth that made her look good. He was in imminent danger of being shot as the messenger.

"Be careful what you wish for, Giselle. Sometimes people ask for the truth and they're totally unprepared for it." He knew the observation was rhetorical. This had to be resolved between them.

She merely raised an eyebrow. "I can handle the truth."

"Did you know Danny and I were best friends?"

She looked startled. Obviously not where she'd expected him to start. "Helene said you played college football together."

"Yeah. Two poor boys getting the shit kicked out of them on the field for a full-ride scholarship. Did it ever strike you as odd that Danny and Helene wound up married so shortly after we divorced?"

A slight frown wrinkled her forehead. "She said Danny felt you'd wronged her and after she was free he realized he'd been in love with her all along." Giselle was quick. Despite the fact that she spoke slowly, the words coming almost reluctantly, he could tell from her deepening frown she was piecing together what had really happened.

"He might've realized he was in love with her then, but they'd both realized they were in lust a little earlier in the game." He stared into her eyes with a steady gaze, willing her to see the truth. "I was in Chicago for a gallery opening. Helene couldn't make it because she had a weekend install." He'd respected her career demands as an interior designer. "I was supposed to stay for dinner with the gallery owner and fly back home the next morning. But when we were on the phone, she told me how much she missed me and how lousy she felt about not making the gallery showing." And he'd felt guilty as hell because rather than missing her, he'd been relieved to be away from the marriage that was a mistake. "I ditched dinner with Jules, the owner, and caught a red-eye back home to surprise her. I've got to tell you, it was one hell of a surprise."

Giselle mouthed a silent *no*, her eyes wide with denial.

He was still angry when he thought about it. "When I walked in that morning, my wife and my best friend were screwing in *my* bed, in *my* house." She uttered a strangled noise and briefly closed her eyes as if that could shut out his words. Ruthlessly, he continued. "Pardon me for not referring to it as 'making love' but it felt like I was getting screwed at the time. I'll spare you the drama and intimate details, but apparently this had been going on for a couple of months. Oddly enough, I didn't feel like climbing into bed with them or even the guest room so I left. I took a cab to a bar, got knee-crawling drunk and proceeded to go home with Lisa the bartender. It wasn't the right thing to do, but it was one night and one time."

Giselle swallowed. "I'd like to think you're lying but you're not, are you?"

"No."

Giselle rubbed one finger against her forehead as if warding off a headache. "I pushed Helene to take the house—" self-derision laced her brief laughter "—to take everything she could in the divorce settlement. She said she just wanted to be fair, but it was because she didn't have a leg to stand on, wasn't it?" Giselle narrowed her eyes. "Was this why you took this assignment? So you could set the record straight?"

"If that was the case, when you made your pointed remark in your office, I could've told you then and walked out. For that matter, I'm sure your parents are still at the same address and you're easy to contact through the magazine. I could've 'set the record straight' at any time." Was it so damn hard for her to think well of him? Apparently.

"So why didn't you?"

"Why would I have done that, Giselle? She's your sister and your parents' daughter. I was the outsider who was going away. And you were married to Barry at the time." Let her make of that what she would. "What purpose would it have served?"

"But you let us all think—"

"I did cheat on her, Giselle. We were still married and I had sex with Lisa. That's an irrevocable truth. It's not the entire, unadorned truth but it did happen."

She shook her head. "I consider that mitigating circumstances. I owe you an apology. Sam McKendrick, I officially apologize for being such a bitch."

She offered her hand across the table. Sam didn't realize until that moment just how much it meant to have her look at him with some measure of respect once again, even though he regretted the latent betrayal and anger he sensed Giselle felt toward Helene.

Sam took her proffered hand, her touch ricocheting through him. Her eyes darkened and she tried to pull her hand away. Instead of relinquishing it, he twined his fingers through hers and leaned further into the table. "I don't think I'm going to be satisfied with just a handshake." He sucked one of her fingertips and felt her quiver. Sweet. Erotic. The urge to kiss his way up her arm shook him. Reluctantly, he released her.

"But we covered that earlier," she said, her voice unsteady. "Your satisfaction or lack thereof isn't my concern." Her mouth said one thing but a carnal hunger glimmered in her eyes.

He didn't want to stop at just kissing his way up her arm. And out of nowhere he realized it didn't have anything to do with him but everything to do with her. He wanted to please her, indulge her, satiate her. Was this what Lisle Gilbreath had meant when she said he'd find clarity through Giselle?

"Then I'll just have to devote myself to *your* satisfaction." He leaned into her, his voice low and intimate, and she automatically responded by leaning toward him, as well. Her scent teased at him across the table as she rimmed her lower lip with the tip of her tongue in a nervous gesture. "Whatever you want, whenever you want it, however you want it."

8

WHATEVER YOU WANT, whenever you want it, however you want it danced through her head like a sensual promise throughout dinner, a backdrop to the sense of betrayal and deception on the part of her sister. If Giselle hadn't pushed Sam, would the truth still lie enshrouded in Helene's half-truths?

"Could I interest either one of you in dessert?" their server, a petite brunette, asked with a winsome smile.

Giselle was surprised Sam hadn't noticed the waitress. He truly seemed to only have eyes for her, which was the stuff of which fantasies were made. Men like Sam didn't overlook pretty women at the bar or a cute little waitress for Giselle. Men like Sam didn't go around pledging themselves to her sexual satisfaction. Heck, for that matter, no man had yet taken that vow, not even her ex-husband.

"Giselle?" She started at Sam's voice, snapping out of her reverie. "Dessert? Coffee?"

"Nothing for me." *Just you.* She mentally slapped herself.

Within minutes they settled the bill, Giselle tucked

away the receipt for her expense account, and they stepped out into the Sedona evening.

Giselle shivered and wrapped the fine wool muffler, a souvenir gift from her parents' summer vacation in Scotland, about her neck. "Burr. The temperature really dropped while we were in there."

"Do you want to wait here and I'll go get the SUV?" Sam offered.

"Thanks, but I'll enjoy the walk and it'll warm me up."

She welcomed the block-and-a-half walk in the night's bracing chill back to the public parking lot that ran behind the shops. Sam's vow had her strung as tight as a Stradivarius. She'd been excruciatingly aware of everything, from the way the light glinted off his hair to the shape of his broad hands with their faint sprinkling of dark hair.

They'd kept the conversation neutral, discussing travel and cooking, but an awareness always hummed between them, a banked fire that burned inside her. There was another fire, born of hurt and anger that Helene had lied to her, to their entire family. Yet Giselle still felt guilty that she wanted Sam when he'd once been Helene's.

It was too much to sort through and she needed some time alone to untangle it all. On the other hand, she didn't want this fantasy night—and that's what it had turned into when he walked into the restaurant, looked at her and declared he wanted her to the exclusion of every other woman—to end. It was just the way she'd fantasized and she wanted to draw out the evening as long as possible. Getting out in the fresh air was precisely what she needed now.

"Nice place," Sam said as they left the adobe-fronted restaurant behind. "I'd definitely eat there again."

Something had shifted, changed between them with the truth about Sam and Helene's marriage out in the open. Her family still wouldn't approve of her being here with him, she still shouldn't be here with him, but she was working through this the best way she knew how.

"Yeah, I liked the food and the music." And the company. "Hey, did you get this one today?"

Giselle pointed to the small statue of the artistically interpreted javelina on the sidewalks. Some cities had the Cows on Parade and she'd heard of Moose on Parade in Canadian cities, but the Sedona sidewalks boasted the javelina, a small animal that looked like a cross between a pig and a wild boar, so ugly it was cute. Sam had been captivated by them earlier today when they'd walked through town, snapping photo after photo of the javelinas.

"I missed this one," Sam said. "We didn't come this far down. I'll have to get it tomorrow."

"It'd make a great Christmas card." She laughed at the Santa hat perched jauntily over one eye of the little statue. She stumbled and even though she was in no danger of falling face-first on the sidewalk, Sam grabbed her elbow to catch her.

"I'm fine." Breathless at his touch, but fine. "Thanks."

He could've moved his hand away, he should've

moved his hand away, but he didn't. She could've shrugged him off, should've shrugged him off, but she didn't. Instead, he slid his hand down her arm and clasped her hand in his. As if of one accord, their steps slowed and they window-shopped the now-closed stores. It felt ridiculously special and intimate to hold hands.

For one second Giselle wanted to stop time to preserve the romanticism of being in this place at this time with this man, his big, masculine hand engulfing hers, his scent wrapping around her, the curl of their breath rising and mingling like smoke in the cold.

"I'd planned on an early evening because I thought with the time change I'd be exhausted, but I'm not," she said. "There's something very energizing about this place." As if to give her words credence, the outline of the red rocks loomed against the distant skyline as they descended into the open-air parking area. "Why don't we head over to the Red Rock Fantasy at Los Abrigados?"

"Red Rock Fantasy? Are you just making that up to drive me crazy?"

Giselle laughed, although her body responded to his sexy growling tone. "It's not *that* kind of fantasy." It had been part of her research. "Each year the twenty-acre resort adjacent to Tlaquepaque hosts a contest. The contestants are a mixture of families and businesses. They're given eight sheets of plywood, two-thousand lights and a theme. The winner wins a membership to the resort or one of its affiliates." She sounded like an infomercial.

Sam, however, seemed thoroughly enchanted. "Cool. If that's what you want to do, I'm up for it."

Giselle knew she should untangle her fingers from his, skip the Red Rock Fantasy, return to the cottage and retreat to her room. She shouldn't be holding hands and flirting and generally pretending Sam wasn't forbidden to her. Darren's analogy came to mind. For once she was going to try on the dress she knew she couldn't have.

They crossed the parking lot and Giselle reluctantly let go of Sam's hand to fish the SUV keys out of her purse. She hit the remote unlock button twice and they climbed in. Inside, the SUV wasn't appreciably warmer than outside. Giselle started the engine. "I'll give it a minute to warm up."

She pushed the control button for the heated leather seats. They'd warm up in no time.

The streetlamp's glow slanted through Sam's window, illuminating part of him, leaving the side of his face closest to her cloaked in shadow. Want arced between them, drew them. Sam turned to her, the breadth of his shoulders blocking the light, plunging them into a dark intimacy.

"Giselle…" He feathered his fingers against her jaw and instinctively she turned her head, pressing a kiss to his palm.

"Sam…"

She didn't try to fight it, didn't want to fight it any longer. Hadn't she known this was inevitable?

He buried his fingers in her hair and his lips captured

hers in a slow kiss that sampled, branded, claimed. She tunneled her hands through his hair and clasped them behind his neck.

She sighed into the warmth of his mouth. It was the sweetest seduction, where she was both the seducer and the seduced. The plying of his lips against hers, the tender, sweeping exploration of her mouth with his tongue. Their kiss grew bolder, deeper, more demanding. She strained toward him, the center console keeping them apart from the neck down.

"Come here," he murmured against her mouth, tugging her toward the passenger side. Perhaps it was the emboldening dark, the unleashing of a passion that had brewed and simmered for years, the fuel of having a long-standing fantasy play out earlier in the restaurant, the faint anger of having been lied to by her sister, the simple fact that in his lap was precisely where she wanted to be, or a combination thereof. Regardless, she climbed over the console while he reclined the passenger seat.

Sam steadied her with his hands at her waist and then pulled her down firmly against him. Her hips settled against his, his thighs cradling her. Finally. She closed her eyes, committing the breadth of his shoulders, the hard plane of his chest, the masculine cradle of his thighs to memory.

His arms enveloped her and the scent that was Sam mingled with her own as he cupped one big hand behind her head and guided her mouth back to his, as if he'd been far too long without her kiss. His need was an almost palpable force.

The hunger in his kiss seared her. Her tongue mated with his and his cock swelled to an even harder, more pronounced ridge where it was nestled between her thighs.

A sweet, hot slickness flooded her. Sam. For now. Just this once, he wasn't Helene's anymore. He was simply Giselle's. Hers.

Their deep, drugging kisses took on a frantic quality. He wrapped his big hands around the curve of her buttocks and kneaded, pulling her tighter, harder against his hard-on. She shamelessly ground against his rigid erection. He thrust up against her and she mewled into his mouth.

She…wanted…him.

So wet. Feels so good. Wanted him so long. So close, so very, very close. Please. Sam, oh, Sam.

Another thrust as his big hands kneaded her buttocks hard and…yes! She came, her orgasm slamming through her.

A sharp rap and a spotlight suddenly appeared at the window.

"Police. Break it up in there."

Giselle bolted upright along with Sam. Sam rubbed at the fog obscuring the passenger window. Sure enough, one of Sedona's finest stood outside, aiming a flashlight inside. Sam put down the window.

The cop shook his head and grinned when he got a good look at them. Giselle supposed they were a little older than the average window foggers. "Why don't you just take this home? You know, we have public decency laws."

"We're not indecent, officer," Sam said, although there was no mistaking his jutting erection in his pants. "Not yet, anyway."

Giselle scrambled back over the console to the driver's seat, her legs still unsteady from the aftermath of her orgasm. "We're just leaving now."

By rights, she should be mortified. She'd just been caught by a cop making out in a parking lot like a teenager with her former brother-in-law. Guilt and mortification be damned; she'd never felt better in her life.

SAM POWERED his window back up as the cop turned and continued policing the parking lot. Giselle began to laugh. "That might've been embarrassing if it wasn't so funny."

Sam grinned despite the fact that his balls ached thanks to near-coitus interruptus. "We're probably a little older than he's used to."

"You think?" she said, throwing the SUV into Reverse. "Actually that qualifies as both funny and embarrassing. You know, just for the record...I don't usually...as a matter of course...."

"Me, either. It's been years. High school."

She certainly was relaxed. Maybe it was tacky to ask, but hell, if she'd had an orgasm and he was the responsible party who'd put that smile on her face, he wanted to know. And he wanted to hear her acknowledge it.

"You sure are relaxed."

"I am. Aren't you?" She made a left out of the parking lot.

"Not particularly." That seemed a more diplomatic answer than saying he was still hard as an iron rod for her. "Did you… You know…"

She quirked an amused smile at him. "Did I what?"

What the hell was wrong with him? Why was he stumbling all over himself? Because it was damn awkward to ask a woman if she'd had an orgasm when he'd dry-humped her, that was why. He usually managed himself with more finesse but she'd felt so good and she'd kissed like a madwoman and he'd momentarily lost his mind. Now, it seemed, his dignity was exiting, as well. What the hell? "Did you…*enjoy* that?"

"Very much." Ha! He knew it. "I've never had a cop show up. It was a novel experience."

Damn Giselle's black, little, sexy soul to hell; she was toying with him.

"Are you still up for the Red Rock Fantasy?" she asked with a devilish smirk.

"I'm definitely still up for whatever fantasy you've got in mind. You're in the driver's seat."

"Good. Here we are." He didn't miss the smile dancing around the corners of her delectable mouth as she turned into the driveway between the adobe walls of Tlaquepaque Village. "We can park here and walk through to Los Abrigados."

The headlights picked out a jaguar mural on a retaining wall facing the parking lot. Primal. Animalistic. It struck a responsive chord in Sam.

Giselle circled the lot, finally finding an empty spot in the far back corner. Sam got out of the SUV. He could use a cold shower. He supposed walking around in the cold night air was the next best thing for taming a hard-on that was still throbbing because the object of his lust was still within touching distance. He reached down and caught her hand in his. He'd liked the way it felt on the walk back from the restaurant earlier and he liked the way it felt now. It at least satiated a measure of the need to touch her and be touched by her that had afflicted him since he'd walked back into that restaurant.

They strolled along the cobblestone streets closed to automobile traffic until they came to the ticket booth. They each bought a ticket and Sam caught Giselle's surreptitious glance at the horse-drawn wagon standing a few feet away. Maybe she wouldn't suggest it because then he'd think she was trying to put them into a romantic setting, but he didn't have any such qualms. Wait. How'd he know that's what she wanted and how'd he know that's why she wouldn't say anything? It didn't really matter, he was running with it.

"Let's take the wagon ride," Sam said. Giselle hesitated. "It'll be fun and we'll be contributing to the local economy. You know you want to."

"Let's do it."

"My treat," Sam said.

"But we can expense it—"

"It's Christmas and it's my treat."

"But you shouldn't—"

"I want to. Would you deny me at Christmas?" Husky, raw, unplanned, the question slipped out.

"No." Her eyes were shadowed and mysterious, and he felt as if they'd both floundered into unchartered territory. "I wouldn't deny you at Christmas."

"Then give me a minute." He stepped over to the wagon ride booth. The woman behind the counter had the lined nut-brown face of a woman who'd spent her life outdoors with horses in the relentless southwest sun. Her nametag read Minnie. He glanced over his shoulder. Giselle had approached the big horse that stood patiently waiting in its traces and stroked its neck. Pleased that he'd anticipated what she wanted, he turned back to the woman behind the counter.

"Two adults for the wagon ride, please."

They exchanged tickets and money. "It'll be about another ten minutes," Minnie said. "We want to give the other wagon a head start. Just enough time to warm up with a hot chocolate from that booth over there." She winked at him. "Or maybe not, now that your lady's started talking to Luke."

Frowning, Sam turned toward Giselle. A tall man with a long dark ponytail wearing a Stetson, jeans, cowboy boots and one of those long duster coats had joined her by the horse. He stroked the horse's neck in a rhythm that echoed Giselle's and smiled down at her. She laughed at something the cowboy said and Sam realized Cowboy Luke rubbed him the wrong damn way.

"Don't worry about Luke," Minnie said, waving a dismissing hand. "No need to be jealous."

"I'm not jealous," Sam automatically protested. He wasn't the jealous type. Even when he'd found Danny and Helene together, he'd felt betrayed and pissed off but never jealous. In fact, more than once during their marriage, he'd thought that maybe Helene found his lack of jealousy disappointing. This guy might be irritating as hell, but Sam certainly wasn't jealous.

"That's good 'cause the only thing Luke might do is talk her to death about horses."

Bullshit. Sam recognized the look on good ole Luke's face and he might be *talking* about a horse but he wasn't *thinking* about a horse. Luke was thinking about the same damn thing Sam had been thinking about all afternoon. Giselle wasn't a flirt, but sexuality rolled off her in waves.

A low-key buzzing filled his head and the amulet grew warm against his chest, the same as it had in the crystal shop. A screen, shimmering with static, appeared in his head, just as it had earlier. Was he really tuning in to Giselle's fantasy?

The scene flashed into focus. *A bale of hay with a southwestern blanket spread over it. Giselle, naked, on all fours, bending over the hay bale, her head thrown back. A man, visible from behind, wearing only a Stetson and leather chaps, gripped her hips and rode her from behind, plunging into her again and again as she rocked back to meet his thrusts, his balls slapping against her.*

What the…? Sam showed up in the Disney-rated fantasy and Cowboy Luke got the X-rated over-a-hay-bale one? Not just *no. Hell no!* Wait. Maybe that wasn't Cowboy Luke, because the fantasy guy didn't have a ponytail. In fact, he had the same hair as Sam. *That* was more like it. But just in case….

"Then I guess I'd better save her from an early death." His smile felt tight on his face as he closed the distance between him and Giselle.

Sam wrapped his arm around her waist from behind, hauling her back against him. He tightened his arm and his cock nestled between her cheeks. He felt her start of surprise, but even stronger was the surge of excitement that sizzled between them. He couldn't deny that while he'd been pissed off he was also very turned on by what was playing out in Giselle's hot little head. "Got the tickets, babe."

He directed his words to Giselle, but he looked straight at Cowboy Luke, just so there'd be no confusion on the other man's part. Sometimes cowboys could be kind of slow.

Luke flashed a screw-you-buddy smile at Sam. "You must be Sam, her photographer."

"Actually, I'm her love slave." Her elbow dug back into his ribs. "You must be Luke the Cowpoke."

"One and the same."

"Minnie suggested a hot chocolate while we wait," Sam said, murmuring in an undertone and tracing his thumb against the indent of Giselle's waist, deliberately closing Luke out of the exchange.

Luke reached into his pocket, pulled out a business card and handed it to Giselle. "Give me a call if I can help you with any research. Maybe you might decide to do a piece on cowpokes. Or if you decide you want a private riding lesson, I'm your man." He flashed his teeth in another smile. Sam wouldn't mind rearranging them for him. Luke would give her riding lessons over Sam's dead body because he had a strong suspicion Luke's riding lessons didn't involve a horse. "I better check the traces. See you back here in a few."

Halfway to the hot cocoa booth, Giselle yanked Sam behind a large shrub and rounded on him. "Babe? We were talking about horses and you blow in like it's a showdown at the OK Corral. And you introduced yourself as my love slave?" Her outrage gave way to mirth. "What were you thinking?"

Sam stabbed his hand through his hair. Maybe he'd sort of acted like a jackass. He didn't know what was wrong with him. This wasn't typical behavior. "Okay. Sorry. He might've been *talking* about horses but I know what he was *thinking* about." *And I know what you were thinking about, too.*

"How could you possibly know what he was thinking?"

"Because I'm a guy and I know what a guy's thinking when he looks at a woman the way he was looking at you." He shook his head, trying to clear it. "Really, I'm sorry. I'm not normally like this."

Her voice softened. "And then you called me babe. I'm not a babe. You must be losing your mind."

"It's a distinct possibility."

9

AN HOUR LATER, exhaustion washed over Giselle.

"I'm done," she said. "I've got to go to bed."

"Did the wagon ride push you over the edge?"

It had been fun, wedged on the wagon's bench seat between Sam and a grandmother from El Paso with her three grandchildren. Giselle and Sam had shared a blanket and being pressed next to him had been an exquisite torture—the next best thing to cuddling, except she'd never particularly considered Sam cuddle material. In her head, she'd always limited him to sexual activity, which he was very good at in her head and even better in person. But once they'd climbed in the wagon, he'd put his arm around her shoulder and she'd wound up tucked against him.

"Hmm, I think relaxing on the wagon ride did me in." The earlier orgasm hadn't hurt in the relaxation department, either. "That and the fact it's almost midnight at home and I hardly slept last night." He quirked a questioning eyebrow her way. "I never sleep well the night before a trip. I'm always worried I'll oversleep and miss my flight." True enough, but she'd also known

Sam was going to show up and he was the *real* culprit behind her sleeplessness.

"Then let's head back. It's been a long day."

They crossed the cobblestone drive to the parking lot. She handed over the rental SUV keys. "You drive." Not only was she tired, but her head was spinning with everything that had happened today. She felt emotionally punch-drunk. And nervous. She was about to go to a romantic cottage with a man who had stated unequivocally that he wanted her, a man she'd had an orgasm with and a man who, no matter how she sliced it or diced it, had once been her brother-in-law.

Once again, the confines of the SUV were close and intimate, and what had happened there a brief hour ago seemed to fill the small space. Out of the corner of her eye, Giselle saw Sam look at her before the dome light turned off. Was he thinking about their earlier parking lot encounter? *Encounter*—that had a nice melodramatic ring to it. She needed space and time to sort through things. She snapped her seat belt into place.

"So, any big Christmas plans?" she asked, infusing a cheery tone into her voice, much as she'd use with a store clerk or some other stranger.

He started the SUV and backed out of the parking space, slanting her a look that said he knew what she was up to.

"Nope. You're heading to your parents'?"

"Yeah, family tradition and everything." For a short period of time, he'd been a part of that. "I'm heading there straight from the airport. Are you going to your mother's? She lives northwest of Atlanta, right?"

"My mother died in February."

"Oh, Sam. I'm so sorry." She instinctively reached over and touched his arm in a gesture of sympathy. "She was a nice lady." Giselle had met her at Sam and Helene's post-elopement wedding reception. She'd been quiet, unassuming, and it had been obvious Sam was her pride and joy. It had been equally obvious she'd found the Randolphs a little intimidating. Heck, they were Giselle's family and sometimes even she found them daunting. Giselle had made it a point to engage Martha McKendrick in conversation. "I'm sure this year has been hard."

"I miss her."

Tears burned the back of her eyes at the loneliness and loss underscoring his simple declaration. Giselle knew from Helene that Sam and his mom were close because it'd just been the two of them when he was growing up.

"Want to talk about it?"

He stared straight ahead at the road. "Nothing to talk about, really. She found out on December 3 she had stage three ovarian cancer and she died on February 29. It's a leap year." He shrugged. "Bad things happen to good people. It was the story of her life. Raising a kid alone, disowned by her family, and finally when she was in a good place in her life, that happened."

Maybe it was a birth-order thing or maybe it was just her personality, but Giselle was a fixer. And she didn't miss the fact that Sam had lumped raising him in there as one of the bad things in his mother's life and that was just wrong. "Sam, I only met her at the reception but we talked. She was so proud of you and she obviously loved you so much. Never ever think you were anything less than a source of joy to her, regardless of what the circumstances of your birth were."

"Thank you." Silence wrapped in private sorrow stretched between them. "She liked you, you know. She said you were the genuine beauty in your family."

The tears that had threatened earlier seeped down Giselle's face. She swiped at them with the back of her hand. "That was a lovely thing to say. I'm sorry I didn't know her better and I'm sorry for your loss."

"Thanks." He pulled into the resort parking lot and killed the engine. Giselle sensed the shift in him; he'd closed the topic. A very selfish part of her was relieved, sorry in fact she'd ever brought the subject of holidays and family up. She didn't want to think of Sam's mother having to suffer. She didn't want to think of Sam alone on Christmas day. She didn't want to know that if her sister hadn't been busy screwing his best friend when they were married that Sam would at least still have her family to fall back on. Maybe he had a girlfriend he'd spend the day with, but she didn't get that impression. He'd sounded as if he would be alone when she'd asked about the day.

Giselle had brushed aside his assertion that the truth could be hard to handle and not knowing was easier, but he was right. Not knowing was much easier.

"I'm sorry Helene did…what she did," she said as they walked along the stone path leading to the cottage entrance. Overhead, the stars shone brightly in the night sky.

"Why should you apologize for your sister?" Sam pulled the room pass card out of his jacket pocket.

"She's my people."

"But you're not responsible for her, Giselle. Unless you encouraged her to have an affair—" He opened the cottage door for her to walk in ahead of him.

"God, no!"

"I didn't think so," he locked the dead bolt and turned back to face her "Which makes you not responsible for what she does or doesn't do."

Giselle felt like a fool. Obviously he thought her an idiot. "You're right. Forget I mentioned it." She headed for her room.

He caught her arm, stopping her. "No. I'm not going to forget it." His blue eyes seemed to see into her very soul. "I'm not going to forget any of tonight." For one heart-pounding second she thought he was going to kiss her again. Instead, he released her. "What time do you want to get started in the morning?"

Give her a second and her heart rate might return to normal now that he wasn't touching her. "I'm planning on breakfast at eight-thirty."

He nodded. "Just so you won't be alarmed if you hear me coming or going, I'll be out the door for a run at six-thirty. I'm usually gone an hour, maybe a little less."

"Thanks for the heads-up." She'd be sure to have her shower over and done with before he got back. Having Darren in the next room while she showered had never mattered. Sam, however, was a far cry from Darren. Better to be naked and wet when he was nowhere on the premises.

"Thought it'd help with coordinating shower times." He grinned. "Unless you need help scrubbing your back."

His thoughts were so close to her own, she felt a tide of red rush up her neck and face. "I'll manage."

"You're welcome to join me on the run if you'd like."

Giselle laughed and walked toward her bedroom. "I'll pass. The only way I'd run was if something was chasing me." She wrapped her hand around the doorknob.

"I could if you wanted me to," he said with a teasing grin that left her kind of light-headed.

"It'd be a very short run. I'll stick with my yoga tape, but thanks for the offer." She stepped into her bedroom.

"Sure thing."

She almost had her door shut when he spoke again. "Just let me know when you're ready for me to chase you."

SAM LEANED FORWARD slightly as he ran up the steep grade on a section of Schnebly Hill, the road parallel to Sedona's Highway 89A. His breath formed white wisps in the air. Below him, to his left, lay the city.

Headlights pierced the early morning dark and the downshift of a truck engine sent him further to the shoulder of the road. He'd been in bed, almost asleep last night, when that static had gone off in his head and the stone amulet had grown warm against his chest, signaling what was apparently going on in Giselle's head.

He'd been hard in less than sixty seconds. But then again, watching her go down on him in her fantasy tended to affect him that way.

They sat in the SUV in the dark corner of the Tlaquepaque parking lot. She leaned over the console and whispered in his ear. "Did you really mean it when you said you wanted to satisfy me when I wanted how I wanted and where I wanted?"

He readily agreed.

"Then lie back."

He reclined in the seat. Giselle unzipped his pants, pulled out Mr. Happy and proceeded to lick, suck, nibble and generally blow his mind.

Boing. Instant boner.

It occurred to him about midway through her fantasy that he could just walk across the living room and knock on her bedroom door. But then what? Just announce, "Here it is, baby. Have a go"?

That didn't seem the best idea since she might be a little pissed that he was tuning in to her private fantasies. He was also very much aware of her response in the restaurant when he'd actually played out the fantasy he'd "read" earlier. She'd had a tough time accepting her fantasy as a reality.

So last night he'd gone for the only viable option. He'd whacked off, doubly aroused by the knowledge that if that particular fantasy was going through her head, she was doubtless doing the same.

He'd discerned one more facet of Giselle Randolph's makeup, through fantasy monitoring. Most women weren't ambivalent about fellatio. They either liked it or were of the get-that-thing-away-from-me variety. He knew with certainty where Giselle stood on the issue.

He dodged a large rock on the shoulder of the road, checked his time and let his mind drift back to Giselle and the amulet.

Were her fantasies coming to him in real time or was there a delay? He was fairly certain it was real time based on the circumstances and timing around his three tune-ins.

And how did any of this translate to clarity for him? If anything, it was confusing as hell.

The tricky part of acting out her fantasies would be not revealing he had the inside track. And there was no doubt that knowing her fantasies was…well, hot, and all the hotter because there was a forbidden element to it. Was that fair to her? Didn't that leave him with a distinct advantage?

He gave his conscience the smackdown. He had three days with her. He'd take whatever advantage he could find in the war to win her heart.

He turned around at what should be the three-mile mark and started the return leg of his workout. He was about two miles out from the cottage when the static started again and the amulet grew warm.

He grinned. And women said men thought about sex all the time? Hell, Giselle fantasized frequently. The woman was into sex. And it was a hell of a turn-on— sort of like watching porn videos starring the two of them.

In a matter of seconds he was tuned in to her sex scenario.

Giselle stepped into the oversized, white-tiled shower in the cottage bathroom. She closed her eyes and tilted her head back in the warm water. Sam appeared and slipped into the shower behind her. She glanced at him over her shoulder and offered a sultry welcoming smile. "Let me pleasure you," he murmured. Another smile granted him permission. Standing behind her, he nuzzled her neck. Sam encircled her with his arms and slid his hands over her ribs to the fullness of her breasts, strok-ing and fondling them while he kissed her neck and shoulder.

Another man slipped into the shower with them. "Your pleasure is my pleasure," he said to Giselle. Sam nearly stumbled on his run. Two was a party, three was a crowd. But then this wasn't his fantasy, was it? And actually, it was interesting, not to mention damn arousing, to discover her erotic hot buttons.

In a show of male territorial pride, he glanced, in his head, at the other guy's equipment. Sam's dick was bigger, if it was actually him in the fantasy and not just his psyche throwing him in there. In fact, he couldn't see the other man's face. Was that Giselle leaving it blank or Sam? Who the hell knew? What a head game mess.

*He and the other man took their time washing her,
he on the left, the other guy on the right. They stroked,
rubbed, massaged with their soap-slicked hands until
no inch of her remained untouched. After they rinsed
away the soap, she sank to the tiled shelf that formed
a seat at one end of the shower, much like a queen
taking her throne. Her eyes glittered and her nipples
puckered against her full breasts. "Wash yourselves,"
she said, "while I watch."*

Sam offered Giselle silent thanks that she wasn't
into homoeroticism, at least not yet. He might have to
yank off the necklace if she'd wanted them to wash one
another.

*After washing and rinsing himself, enshrouded in
steam, Sam kissed his way down her body until he knelt
in front of her. He nudged her legs further apart and
buried his face between her thighs while his counter-
part devoted himself to pleasuring her breasts, then
they switched places.*

While Sam didn't want to share her in real time—
share her, he hadn't even had her himself—he had to
admit it was one hot fantasy.

*Sam rolled her nipples between his fingertips and
tugged. Wrapping her hand around his cock, she began
to stroke him. She tugged him closer and took him in
her mouth while the other guy pistoned in and out
between her thighs.*

He watched it play out in his head and had no sense
of touch or taste, but he could swear he felt the sweet,
hot wetness of her mouth wrap around his cock as he ran.

His erection muted the cries of her orgasm as she came. He withdrew from her mouth and came across her breasts while the other man spurted across the soft mound of her belly.

Ho-ly shit! He sprinted as if his life depended on it. If he could get back to the cottage before she finished the shower, before she left the bathroom, if he could catch her in the final throes of her fantasy… He ran harder and faster than he had in years.

He fumbled the key card into the slot and then flung the door open, banging it against the wall. The bathroom stood empty. Damn. He closed the cottage door behind him and leaned forward, his hands braced on his knees, trying to catch his breath and some small measure of sanity.

"Sam?" Giselle called from behind her closed bedroom door.

"Yeah…it's me," he said, gasps punctuating the words. He hadn't run so hard since he'd played college ball. He was getting too old to move like that.

She opened her door and stepped into the den, tugging a sweater into place over her hips. "Is everything okay?"

He straightened. The urge, the absolute necessity of bringing her pleasure, of fulfilling at least a portion of her fantasy, overwhelmed him, obliterating reason and caution. He didn't know what the hell this had to do with his own clarity, and at the moment, he just didn't give a damn. He wanted to make love to her, to bring her to orgasm until she wept with pleasure.

"That—" he grabbed the edge of his sweatshirt and T-shirt and pulled them up over his head and dropped them to the floor "—depends on you."

10

It was a little mind-boggling to have the object of her fantasies walk in the door, declare it was up to her whether everything was okay and rip off his shirt. And thank goodness he was alone because if there was some kind of magic at work and her fantasies were about to play out…well, she might daydream about two men at once, but she didn't ever want to actually do that. It just made her really, really hot to think about it. She'd been relieved to read once in a magazine survey that she was in the majority of women who fantasized about sex with two men at once but really only wanted one in bed with her when it came right down to it. That's what fantasies were for.

He stalked toward her and she swallowed hard, her heart threatening to thump out of her chest.

"Me?"

He stopped a few feet in front of her. "You." Sweat glistened on his skin and darkened his hair where it lay against his neck. Muscles defined his shoulders, arms and chest, and he boasted a nice flat belly without that grossly ripped mutant look. Brown hair was scattered over his chest and trailed down his belly to disappear beneath the edge of his gray sweatpants. A carved, stone disc hung about his neck, suspended on a leather cord. Masculine, elemental, erotic. "Do you want me?"

His question, stark and direct, shimmered between them, a mix of challenge, arrogance and a hint of uncertainty. Giselle took a deep breath to center herself. This was it. The moment of truth. If she said no, it was a lie and regret was sure to follow. If she said yes, it was a betrayal and regret was sure to follow. She'd spent two years trying to forget about Sam but wanting him nonetheless. How could she walk away from him now? If he was still married to Helene, she'd have no choice, but he wasn't and she did. The same way her sister had had a choice in presenting half-truths. *Do you want me?* Only with every fiber of her being for two long years.

Sedona obviously was about magic and change and she had three days counting today because whatever was going on now wouldn't come her way again. This was time out of place and space, and she'd deal with the aftermath later.

She exhaled and tangled her gaze with his. "Yes." Her mouth was dry and the single word came out almost a whisper. She swallowed, her heart thudding heavy against her ribs. "How could I not want you, Sam McKendrick?"

His slow smile and the sexual promise in his hooded blue eyes fanned the heat low in her belly. "Well, I'm sweaty." With a few steps, he closed the gap between them, bracing his arms against the wall on either side of her. She leaned against the wall, not to get away from him but for support because her knees weren't fully operational with Sam so close.

It was far from off-putting. Muscles corded his arms on either side of her. There was something unutterably sexy about the dark masculine hair of his underarm. "I like sweaty."

Insecurity, however, reared its ugly head. She clenched her hands at her sides because once she touched him she'd be beyond the point of no return. Straightening her spine against the unyielding wall, she posed the two questions she *had* to ask. "Why me, Sam? Is this to get back at Helene?" Why else would gorgeously sexy half-naked Sam McKendrick be interested in plain-Jane Giselle Randolph?

"This has nothing, absolutely nothing to do with your sister. And the only way she'll ever know is if you tell her. That's your call." He leaned down, angling his head to nuzzle just below her ear. *Oh, yes.* "I really don't want to talk about Helene any longer. She's not part of my equation." He scraped his teeth over the sensitive tip of her earlobe, sending a delicious shiver through her.

Oh, God, she couldn't think clearly with his bare chest right in front of her, his scent surrounding her, his warm breath gusting against her hair, his mouth on her ear and neck.

"Why you?" he continued, pushing away from the wall to stand before her. "I wish I knew. Honestly, I wish I didn't want you." He plowed his hand through his damp hair, standing it on end. Sexy in a goofily endearing kind of way. "It would make everything a whole lot easier if it was someone else. But I walked into your parents' kitchen two years ago…" He shook his head as if still trying to clear it from an impact. "I told you last night, heaven help us both, but I want *you*."

Like the breaking of a dam, his words unleashed the want, the need, the craving, the hunger she'd contained for so long. Nothing mattered except her, him, and this moment.

She'd run from her attraction to Sam two years ago and she'd been running ever since. And it would be far easier to keep running if she didn't know her sister had cheated on Sam first. Could she really be faulted for giving up the race?

She settled her palms against his damp, hair-roughed chest. She slid her hands up over his chest to his heavy shoulders, leaning in to lick a lazy path along his collarbone. His skin tasted salty beneath the tip of her tongue. She trailed tiny kisses along his stubbled jaw, aroused by the slight abrasion against her cheek and lips. His big body quivered in response and a purely feminine thrill shot through her that she affected him so. No going back now, no more denial. "If you want me, then have me."

FOR ONE BRIEF SECOND he wavered. He really was a selfish bastard when it came right down to it. While his ex-wife wasn't part of his equation, she was a very significant part of Giselle's world. Giselle might have struggled with what had happened last night, but now… He could try to convince himself she didn't have to mention it to Helene, but he realized with a bone-deep certainty that sleeping with him would eat at Giselle until she "confessed" to her sister.

But she was a grown woman who made her own decisions. And what about the amulet? He hadn't asked for it, hadn't even been looking for it. Wasn't he supposed to bring her pleasure? And she had been the one designated to give him clarity.

And all that aside, he wanted her with a desperation, an ache, that he'd never known before. If she'd said no, he would've respected her decision, but she hadn't. And God help him, he wasn't sure if he was man enough to walk away from her touch, her sweet mouth on his skin, and her "have me," even knowing he was complicating her life immeasurably. He gave her one final out. "Are you sure?"

"I'm sure."

What the hell was wrong with him? He'd come for her. Silently he hauled her up to him and kissed her slowly, thoroughly. Last night in the SUV had been frantic; now he wanted to make it perfect for her. Her hands roamed over his shoulders and beneath his arms to knead his back. He groaned. Had anything ever felt as good as her hands on his bare skin?

He explored her mouth's sweet, wet recesses with his tongue. He cupped her buttock in one hand, a perfect fit, and slid the other hand beneath the hem of her sweater to her silken nakedness. He didn't even try to contain yet another groan. She felt so good.

He plied his fingers along her soft skin to her satin-covered breast. He broke the kiss and nuzzled her jaw. "You said you don't mind sweaty but I stink and I don't want to stink for you." Her hair tickled against his nose. "Come get in the shower with me."

She laughed, running her fingers up and down his back. "You just want to put me to work washing your back."

"Hmm. My back wasn't exactly what I had in mind." He nipped her neck and she quivered in his arms.

"Ah, a wicked mind. I like the way you think."

He licked the spot he'd just nipped. "You might've missed a few spots," he said, dragging his tongue along the juncture of her neck and shoulders, "that I could take care of for you."

"I think we could work out a trade." She sobered, leaning back to look up at him. "Sam, do you have any health issues I should know about?"

"No. I'm careful. I'm selective. And I get checkups regularly. You?"

"I'm good to go. And just for the record, I take a birth control shot once every three months."

"That's good to know." He grabbed her and kissed her hard while he walked her across to the bathroom. "That's just to get you back on track now that we've covered the necessary stuff."

He reached inside the shower and turned the water on. "Why don't we give it a minute to warm up? What temperature do you prefer?"

"I like it hot."

"Something for both of us then. I like it wet."

GISELLE PULLED her sweater over her head. She'd never been particularly modest, yet now, undressing in front of Sam, a sudden onslaught of nervousness left her feeling vulnerable. Maybe it was the stripping away of layers, the exposure, baring herself both literally and figuratively.

"Wait," he said, his voice hoarse, choked.

She paused. "What?"

"Honey, just let me look for a minute." He devoured her with his gaze.

She flushed, hotter still, beneath his incendiary look. "Are you okay?"

"No, baby, I'm not okay. I haven't been okay since the first time I saw you." He closed the gap between them. "No, I'm not okay—" his smile was one hundred percent hot male approval "—I'm great, and I can't believe you have on this red bra." He slid one scorching fingertip along the edge of the red satin cup, his voice hoarse. "Baby, I walked into your mama's kitchen and you stood up and you had on a hot red bra under a T-shirt that said I Brake For Elves and you were the sexiest woman I'd ever seen."

"Are you serious?" He remembered that detail? He'd thought she was the sexiest woman ever? Her heart raced and she trailed her finger along the bra edge, following his earlier route.

"Do I look like I'm kidding?" His raspy voice stroked her.

Feeling wicked and sexy, she glanced down at his erection jutting like a flag pole at the front of his sweats. "You look pretty serious to me."

He hooked his fingers beneath her bra straps and slowly dragged them down her shoulders. "I have dreams about you in a red bra. You, honey, are a dream come true."

She caught his hands. "Hold that thought, big boy, because if you like the bra, you're going to love these." Her hands trembled as she unbuttoned, unzipped and dropped her slacks to the floor. Gooseflesh raced across her skin as she stood before Sam clad in her red push-up bra and green bikini briefs imprinted all over with red ho-ho-ho's.

She was something of a perfectionist and she knew her body was far from perfect—she carried an unfortunate extra ten pounds around her middle. No slender waist for her no matter how much yoga she practiced. However, Sam's hiss of indrawn breath and the frank appreciation in his hooded eyes vanquished her self-consciousness. She was a sexy, powerful woman, imperfections and all.

He chuckled, his eyes hot and glittering. "You are still the sexiest woman I've ever seen…now take it off." His low, hoarse request intensified the ache between her thighs to a throb of need. She reached behind her back.

"Yesterday…on the way from the airport…I was thinking about your breasts…wondering what they looked like, felt like."

She unfastened the back of her bra and slid it off.

Hooking her fingers in the elastic edge, she pulled her panties down and stepped out of them. "Your turn."

Without looking away from her, his gaze hot and hungry, he toed off his running shoes and made quick work of taking off his socks.

Her mouth was dry with anticipation. "Take it off," she said, echoing his earlier request.

He hooked his thumbs in his sweatpants and stopped. "Have you ever thought about me naked?"

"Yes, as a matter of fact." More times than she could count.

"Good."

He pulled off his sweats and underwear and tossed them next to the door.

Lean hips, muscular thighs and a thatch of dark hair that showcased the ridged length of his cock. Oh. My.

He gestured toward the shower. "I think it's hot."

She stepped in. "I know it's wet."

And that was an understatement. Less than half an hour ago she'd been standing in the shower, masturbating to an imagined ménage à trios, and now she was in the shower with Sam…Sam, her forbidden fantasy. If this was another one of those maddening dreams that sometimes taunted her, she didn't want to wake up until she'd known his touch, his taste, his possession.

He stepped into the shower behind her, wrapping his arms around her and pulling her against the solid wall of his body—just like in her fantasy. His erection snugged between her buttocks and all thoughts distilled down to flesh against flesh. She leaned back, absorbing the sensation of his arms encircling her and his solid presence behind her.

If she died here, right now, she'd die happy. He found her neck with his mouth and cupped her breasts in his big hands. Okay, so let's not be hasty with the dying happy thing. A soft moan escaped her and she instinctively ground her buttocks against him and arched her breasts more firmly into his hands.

"Kiss me," he said, half command, half plea. She turned her head, meeting his lips with her own as he tugged her eager nipples between his fingers. She was drowning in sensation.

Her tongue dueled with his and the tension inside her coiled tighter and tighter. This wasn't just any man, and it wasn't just a meeting of flesh. This was Sam, her Sam. She reached over her head, winding her arm around his neck, and kissed him harder, tangling her tongue with his and claiming him.

He turned her around in his arms and backed her up until the back of her legs bumped the shower stall seat. He gently pushed her until she was sitting.

"Give me a minute to clean up."

She leaned her head back against the tiled shower wall and watched as he lathered up. He was a big man—tall, broad-shouldered with well-formed biceps and a nice play of muscle across his shoulders and back. His hair, weighted by the water, hung a shade darker to his shoulders.

He soaped his underarms and down the expanse of his hair-roughed chest to the flat plane of his belly. Her heartbeat thumped against her ribs and seemed to echo in an answering pulse between her thighs.

Slowly, deliberately he wrapped his soapy hand around the length of his penis, long and thick, with a sleek crown. Giselle willed herself not to take over for him then and there. Instead, there was titillation, a separate excitement in waiting.

He cupped his heavy sac in his other hand and she caught her lower lip between her teeth. God, she wanted him.

She tore her hungry gaze from his jutting erection to the heavy-lidded heat of his blue eyes. He stepped back and water coursed over him, rinsing away the soap.

She was so hot and so wet, and it had nothing to do with the steam rising from the shower. The only sound in the glass-fronted enclosure was the steady fall of the water against the tiled floor and the much less steady mingling of her and Sam's breathing.

With a smile that made her thankful for the support of the tiled seat, Sam knelt at her feet. He put one big hand on each of her knees and then slowly slid his palms up her wet thighs.

"I want to see you." His husky voice stroked through to her very core. He parted her thighs and slipped her legs over his shoulders, her knees and calves resting against velvet water-slicked skin and sleek muscles.

"Beautiful," Sam intoned, low and quiet, almost reverent. He leaned forward and paused, his face pressed intimately against her slick folds. She felt his inhalation, as if he was committing her intimate scent to memory.

And then he delicately plied his tongue along her outer lips and everything distilled to the sensation between her thighs.

"Sweet. So very sweet."

His tongue intimately explored her, licking, sucking, nipping, stroking against her pearled clit until she thought she might drown in her own desire. She tightened her legs against his back, drawing him more firmly to her. One minute she didn't think she could take what his mouth was doing to her without truly losing her mind and the next she was desperate he might stop. She grasped her last, quickly disappearing thread of sanity and pushed him away. Last night she'd orgasmed without him. Not today.

"Is something wrong?" he asked, getting to his feet.

"No. Everything is very right." She skimmed her hands over his thighs, defined by muscle and a smattering of dark masculine hair. She wrapped her hands around his lean hips and slowly drew him forward.

"But this is about pleasing you," he said.

"You have no idea how much this is about to please me." Leaning forward, she scattered tiny nibbling kisses down his velvet length. His entire body tensed as rigid as his cock and his groan bounced off the tiled walls. She liked oral sex and was particularly partial to fellatio. How many times had she fantasized about this very thing—Sam in her mouth, the taste of him against her tongue as she pleasured him? Countless.

She'd waited what felt like forever for this, and she wasn't about to rush now. She made love to his cock with her mouth, her need for him growing to a ravening hunger as she tasted a drop of his salty essence and breathed in his musky scent. His heavy balls tightened in her hand. Much as she had earlier with him, he pushed her away.

"Giselle…babe…no…I…" His frantic state matched her own. She knew just how he felt, just what he meant.

Panting, she slid up him and raised one leg in a singular fluid motion. They were definitely on the same wavelength. He hooked his arm beneath her knee and wrapped his other arm around her to support her. She grabbed onto his shoulders.

"Yes, yes, yes," she panted, and then he was in her, stretching her, filling her, and it felt so good she nearly cried. And it was so much more than inserting Tab A in Slot A. She could swear a vibrant aura shimmered around them.

She was prey to a longing only he could satisfy.

"Giselle—" he gasped as his mouth descended on hers, ravishing her. She ravished in return.

Harder, faster until she let go of her last restraint and freed herself to fly apart with Sam to a place she'd never been before, where body, soul, and spirit joined as one, a place uniquely theirs.

CONTENTMENT WASHED over him. He'd had good sex before and there was always the pleasure of coming, but this had been…this had been making love with Giselle.

They'd managed to make their way from the shower to the bedroom and now he fell back into his unmade bed, pulling her down on top of him. In the next room, Giselle's cell phone went off. She immediately tensed.

"Helene?"

"Yeah." She rolled off him and to her side, sitting up. He propped on one elbow.

Helene being out of the picture had been extremely short-lived. "Do you two talk every day?"

He just wanted to know because he might have to conveniently "lose" Giselle's phone if his ex-wife phoned that often. Her presence, even via cell phone, had a way of squelching things between him and Giselle.

"No. Usually once a week."

"You know, I think she knew something neither one of us did." Because he couldn't seem to help himself, he reached over and drew an imaginary circle on her hip. He felt the small quiver his touch elicited and it was… well, exciting to realize how responsive she was to him. What had he been saying? Oh, yeah. "Remember the Christmas she and I were married and you and I polished off that bottle of wine?"

"I remember."

"Did she ever mention that to you?" He skimmed his hand up over her ribs to the fullness of one creamy globe.

She arched her back, opening herself to more of his touch. "Not specifically, no. Why?"

He circled a small, sexy-as-hell beauty mark between her breast and her shoulder. She made a soft purring sound in the back of her throat, also sexy as hell. "She was jealous of you that night."

"Helene was jealous of me? That doesn't make sense. She's beautiful. She never even had the good grace to go through that awkward teenage stage. She was stunning when she wore braces!"

"I'm not making it up and I sure as hell didn't imagine it. She was an unbecoming shade of green. She suggested I might've married the wrong sister."

"How ridiculous."

She didn't have to sound quite so adamant about it. And he wasn't spending any more of their time together discussing Helene. "What's ridiculous is that we're wasting this time." He rolled flat on his back. "Come here."

She came. He loved that she wasn't shy or tentative in bed. She was comfortable with her carnality. "But it's ridiculous she'd—"

Helene needed to get the hell out of the bed with them. He knew enough about Giselle to know she wasn't a passive partner and he cut her off in mid-sentence. "Get on your knees and come here."

He tugged her up his body until she straddled his face, her musky scent intoxicating. The photographer in him saw her as an exotic, erotic flower unfurling. White, creamy thighs. A thatch of dark, curling hair. And at the center a deep pink blossom, glistening with dew.

As a man, he saw her as a woman, his woman, ready for him.

11

THE COTTAGE PHONE rang next to the bed and Giselle answered since she was closest.

"This is the front desk. We have an express delivery package for Mr. McKendrick. Would he prefer us to deliver it to the room or hold it at the desk for pickup?"

"Let me check," Giselle said. She turned to Sam and relayed the information.

"I'll go pick it up and then I can check it over before we head out."

"Hold it at the desk, please," she told the woman on the other end of the line. "Thanks."

She hung up and watched with unabashed pleasure as Sam rolled out of bed, pulled on his briefs and then a pair of jeans. "You're a beautiful man, with or without clothes."

He grinned, obviously pleased she liked the way he looked, and shrugged his broad shoulders into his shirt and began buttoning it. "You're going to make me blush, ma'am."

Right. She angled her head to one side and tapped a considering finger against her cheek, "You know, I definitely prefer you naked. It seems a shame to hide all that muscled flesh." She offered an exaggerated sigh as he tucked his shirt into his jeans.

He grabbed the sheet and pulled it down, leaving her naked on the mattress. "It's a definite shame to cover this flesh," he said, trailing his fingertip along the sensitive inside of her knee, and she dropped her legs apart, open to his gaze. His eyes darkened and his face tightened and just that quick she was wet for him again.

He stepped back. "I'm going to leave while I still can," he said, his voice thick. He cleared his throat, "It's a contract agreement for a gallery showing in San Francisco next year," he added, by way of explanation for the package delivery. "That's what my assistant called about last night."

He started toward the bedroom door and then turned, crossing back to the bed to press a quick, but thorough, kiss to her lips. "I'll be right back."

"No hurry," she said. "This morning's schedule is loose."

She waited until she heard the cottage door close before she climbed out of bed. His sheets smelled like him.

She headed to the bathroom and picked her scattered clothes up from the floor. Maybe sleeping with Sam hadn't been the brightest move she'd ever made. At least he could've had the decency to be lousy in bed. That would've been a bit awkward but ultimately better in the long run.

She pulled on her bra and panties. Then it'd be easy. "Let's just work together, we gave it a try and we're not exactly compatible, so let's just forget about it and move forward on the project." It seemed a cruel stroke of fate that the one man she should be running in the opposite direction from was even better in the flesh than he'd been in her fantasies.

She put on jeans next, and finally tugged her sweater over her head. Even more dangerous was that tender kiss just now before he left. Hot sex followed by bone-melting tenderness and yet the readiness for more hot sex was a dangerous combination.

She'd never had a man so in tune with her. It was uncanny and a little unnerving that their first time making love was almost exactly, except for the third party and the wrap-up at the end, what she'd fantasized. Sam seemed to intuitively know what she liked, what turned her on, what sent her spiraling out of control.

And spiraling out of control was both heady and scary. And this was all very strange, and she didn't know how in the heck she was supposed to handle it.

She'd had sexual relationships before but they'd always followed a pattern. She met a guy, she dated, at some point they made the decision to sleep together and things progressed from there. There was an unspoken couple aspect going on.

This…this…*thing* between her and Sam wasn't defined. They weren't dating. They could never be a couple. The idea of her showing up with her sister's ex-husband was a recipe for familial disaster.

Like an unwelcome item in Pandora's Box, a thought reared its ugly head: how'd she stack up against Helene in bed?

She dragged her brush through her hair and paced over to the fireplace, pursued by the demons of insecurity that came from living with a beautiful sister. How could she not wonder? Giselle knew she had the overachiever syndrome that came with being the oldest, which also included a competitive streak a mile wide.

So, she wasn't beautiful like Helene, but hadn't Sam said Giselle was the most beautiful bride he'd ever seen? Bar none? But was she better in bed? She didn't *want* to think it—knew she shouldn't go there—but she just couldn't help herself. Yes, Sam had probably compared them.

Whether it was right or wrong, she compared men. She'd award Sam five gold stars, not that she had a whole lot to compare him with.

And this was why she didn't do well with casual sex. She wanted to be adored and revered. Not in some weird stalkerish way but because she didn't want to be a convenient, she'll-do-because-another-isn't-available partner. She wanted to be the woman that was wanted above all others. Unfortunately, she wasn't the type who inspired slavish devotion. Longing looks had never come her way. Family vacations to the beach had been downright painful as Helene fended off attention left and right and Giselle simply watched. Was it wrong, shallow to want that for herself? Laughable was more like it.

Her cell phone rang, startling her. Her mother's ring tone. She pushed aside the guilt that crowded her and hurried to answer. It was better to take the call while Sam wasn't around. Infinitely better.

"Hi, Mom." Giselle checked her watch. It was frightfully early in Atlanta, but her mother was an insomniac at best and insane during the holidays.

"Hi, honey. I know you're at work but where'd we put the green serving platter last year?"

Giselle squeezed her eyes shut momentarily. She loved them but, honestly, her family could drive her nuts sometimes. They called her about everything. "Top shelf on the right-hand side of the pantry—"

A sharp rap on the cottage door interrupted her. Had Sam forgotten his entry card? God, please don't let it be Sam. "Look, Mom, let me call you back," she said, hurrying out of her bedroom, "someone's at the door."

"No. I'll hold while you answer it and don't you dare open it without knowing who it is."

Giselle thought about hanging up, but that would send her mom into a panic. She stood on tiptoe to peer through the peephole. "It's the bellhop who brought my luggage yesterday. I'm not sure what he wants. Let me call you back."

"I'll hold." Her mother's voice brooked no argument.

Crap. Giselle silently cursed herself for all the times she'd told her mother she'd call back and hadn't, thus fostering her mother's I'll-hold insistence. "Okay. Hang on a minute, then." She opened the door, "Yes?"

"An overnight package arrived for Mr. McKendrick." He thrust a thick envelope in her direction. "I thought he might need it right away."

"Thanks, I'll take it." She'd told them to hold it. Apparently that message had gotten lost in translation.

Giselle closed her eyes. There wasn't a chance in hell her mother had missed that. The woman had radar ears. Of all the bad timing...

Her mother gasped in her ear and then found her voice. "He just said McKendrick. I know he did. I just heard him say McKendrick. That...that...that cheat Sam is there with you? What's going on, Giselle?"

"Are you okay, ma'am?" the bellhop asked.

She opened her eyes just in time to see Sam sauntering up the steps behind the bellhop. And she'd thought it was bad timing before.

"Everything okay?" Sam said, and then noticed the package in the bellhop's hand. "There it is." He grinned, "Which would explain why they couldn't find it at the front desk."

Giselle stood mute, frozen to the spot as things deteriorated from bad to worse.

"Oh, my God," her mother screeched. "I heard him. It's that snake, Sam. What in the name of all that's holy are you doing there with Sam McKendrick, Giselle?"

They'd hit rock bottom when her mother summoned "in the name of all that's holy." And so much for breaking the news during the after-Christmas dinner cleanup.

In the meantime, Sam pulled a five-dollar bill out of his pocket and tipped the bellhop. "Can you hold on for just a moment, Mother?"

"Oh. It's your mother?" Sam looked as awkward as Giselle felt. "Give her my regards."

"His regards? I think not after what he did to my poor daughter and embarrassed our entire family. You tell him I wouldn't spit on him if he was on fire."

"She says hello," Giselle said weakly.

"I most certainly did not."

Sam raised a mocking eyebrow and stepped past Giselle, "I'll just go open my package in my room and give you some privacy."

Giselle closed the cottage door, barely resisting the urge to bang her head against the unrelenting wood.

"Giselle Simone Randolph, I'm still waiting for an explanation." In her mind's eye, Giselle pictured her mother tapping her foot expectantly.

Giselle retreated to her bedroom, closing the door behind her. She'd prefer to keep the conversation as private as possible. She gave her mother the rundown on Sam standing in for Darren.

"You should have told your boss it was an impossible situation. He should have brought in someone else for you to work with or you should have boycotted the assignment."

"Mom, come on. It would have been very unprofessional for me to do that." Yeah, like it was so professional when she'd sat on his face half an hour ago. She knew she was turning a dull red just thinking about it. It was a good thing she wasn't standing in front of her mother.

"It's just tacky that he showed up to work with you after what he did to us. But I suppose I shouldn't be surprised by such a lack of good taste on his part."

Giselle crossed to her bedroom window and tugged

the curtain aside. She could use the solace of her red-rock view. Whether it was all in her head or had some basis in reality, a calm descended on her. "He has bills to pay just like the rest of us, Mom. It's just another assignment."

"Your father's going to have a coronary." Her mother paused. "Does Helene know? She must not or she would have said something to me. I know she's going to be upset. You shouldn't have done this, Giselle."

This was going even worse than she'd anticipated. And good grief, this was her mother's reaction and they were only talking about her *working* with Sam. "Mom, we're working together, it's not as if we eloped." Where had *that* come from? She hated it when her mouth ran faster than her brain.

"That's not funny, Giselle. You should be more respectful of how upsetting this is."

"It was a bad joke, Mom." How about a *stupid* joke? "I realize you're upset, but for me to work with Sam for four days out of a lifetime isn't such a big deal in the scheme of things." And while her mother wouldn't really see it that way, in the scheme of a lifetime, sleeping with him wasn't that big of a deal, either, was it? Well, okay it was. Never mind.

"I just don't like it. I wish you'd told me."

"It was a sudden thing." Sometimes Mom missed the pertinent details when she was excited or upset. It was worth covering one more time. "I didn't know until two days before we were flying out and I didn't see the point in upsetting you."

"I know you've been excited about this assignment,

honey." Her mom's voice came across much less strident. "I'm so sorry he had to ruin it for you."

"It's fine, Mom. Honest. I think we were all so angry with him that we forgot he's not all bad and he was part of our family at one time."

Her mother sniffed delicately on the other end of the line. "He could've still been part of our family if he hadn't messed around on your sister."

Giselle cringed inside. She'd had the same outlook, but it hadn't been the whole picture. "You know there are two sides to every story and no one ever really knows what goes on within a marriage."

"What are you saying? You were angrier with him than any of us were."

"His mom died this February," Giselle said. There was no way to ease into that kind of update.

"Oh." The lingering edge of anger disappeared completely from her mother's voice. "I'm sorry to hear that. She and Sam were close, and Martha was always sweet to Helene. What happened?"

Giselle filled her in.

"That's terrible. It doesn't change what he did to Helene, but losing her must have been hard on him. It was terrible for your dad when Gran passed on."

"I know. And Daddy had all of us."

"Well, I'm sorry to hear about his mother but I still wish he wasn't there with you."

"Would you spit on him now if he was on fire?" Giselle teased, digging around in her purse until she found the small tin of mints. She was out of gum.

"Hmph." Another joke gone flat. "Do you want me to tell your sister?"

Tempting as it was to let her mother deal with Helene's initial upset, that really wasn't fair to her mom and then Giselle also would have to field what could be a semihysterical phone call. Plus, she and her sister were going to have a discussion about Helene's duplicity and that needed to happen face-to-face.

"Thanks, Mom, but no. I'll tell her when I get home. And it's not as if we'll be teaming up in the future. It's just a one-time thing." She popped two mints in her mouth.

Her mother sighed heavily. "I guess there's no real harm in a three-day assignment. You need to have a word with your editor when you get back about any future assignments, though. This family doesn't need any more trouble from Sam McKendrick."

SAM STAYED in his room until he heard the water running in the bathroom. This was already awkward enough for Giselle without him overhearing her conversation. He'd heard Isobel's declaration she wouldn't spit on him if he was on fire. It had been damn near impossible not to hear. And yeah, he'd known he wouldn't be their favorite person, but it had stung all the same.

He'd liked Ford and Isobel. They were good people, even if they were a little uptight about what other people thought about them. Ford had been as close to a father figure as he'd ever known. He'd thought once or twice about picking up the phone and calling them after his mother died, but even through mind-numbing grief his better sense had prevailed. Apparently, he'd made the right choice.

He stepped out of his bedroom into the den at the same time Giselle exited the bathroom.

"Everything okay?"

"Just peachy." Her strained smile didn't meet her troubled eyes.

Shit. This was all his fault. He gathered her in his arms, holding her against his chest. She stood stiff but he held on to her and in a second or two she relaxed. He offered a silent sigh of relief. Giselle, the one everyone counted on to be strong for them, the problem solver, the glue that held her family together, leaned on him. Of course, if he hadn't put her in this position, she wouldn't need his support now, would she? He rubbed her back. "I'm sorry, Giselle. I'm so sorry I ever came."

She raised her head from his chest, a valiant glint of humor in her eyes. "Which time?"

He laughed but pressed the issue nonetheless. "I'm serious."

Speaking of him coming to Sedona… "You know," she said, "I never got the chance to ask Darren. How did you wind up here?"

He gave her the condensed version of how Darren had contacted him under the guise of discussing a gallery piece but ultimately to pass along news of Giselle's divorce and to let Sam know she was interested in him.

"He told me he was subtle," Giselle said.

"As a brick. I called, you didn't call back, and that's when I decided I had to do something desperate."

"And?"

"I called Darren and offered him money to sub an assignment to me."

Giselle gaped. "You *paid* him so you could come to Sedona with me?"

He couldn't tell if she was flattered or outraged, or maybe a little of both. He traced the upturn of her snub nose. "No. I offered him money. He turned it down. He said this was gratis."

"How much did you offer him? I guess if my company is being bought and sold, I at least want to know my asking price."

He named the sum and her jaw dropped. "You'd pay that much to be here with me?"

"Absolutely. I was prepared to double it if I had to. Desperate men take desperate measures." He sobered. Looking down into her face, he trailed his finger along the gentle curve of her cheek. "I wanted time with you when we were both unattached. I wanted to see if what I'd felt for you, what I thought you'd felt for me, was real."

She pressed a kiss to his wrist as he continued, and he couldn't seem to stop, the words pouring out of him.

"Watching my mother die," he paused and shook his head to clear the memory of how ravaged she'd been by the time death released her from her pain, "I realized… it definitely provides perspective on mortality. And I realized that when it's all over it's the chances you didn't take that you regret, not the ones you did. I didn't want you to be the chance I didn't take. But I didn't stop to think how this would ripple through your family and I should have."

She dropped her gaze to his throat and he could no longer see her eyes, but she didn't pull away from his touch. It was self-defeating, really, to be exploring the lines of her face with his fingertip while apologizing for screwing things up for her, but he couldn't seem not to. He traced the no-nonsense arch of her eyebrow to her temple. "I didn't think last night about how much I was complicating things for you but I did this morning and I still didn't have the willpower not to—"

"Stop," she said, glancing up again and pressing her finger against his lips. "I'm not sorry. Not yet, anyway. I'm a big girl and I knew what I was getting into."

Without forethought, he drew her fingertip into his mouth, laving it with his tongue. Instant heat. Instant desire.

She pressed against him, grinding against his crotch, which immediately expressed interest. "My only regret is that we actually have a job to do and can't stay here all day."

He ground back. "What would you do if we were here all day?"

She widened her eyes in mock innocence. "I'd recommend screwing until we're exhausted, sleeping and then waking up to repeat the vicious cycle."

For a split second he was speechless—turned on, but speechless. He laughed even as his cock hardened. "Don't hold back, babe."

She smiled, sliding her hand down between them to

stroke him. "What can I say? I like sex. I particularly like it with you. Is that off-putting to you?"

"Is that a trick question?"

"Some men can't deal with it."

"Let me guess, your ex-husband—Fred, Harry, what's his name?"

She laughed, "Barry. And yes, he found it a little off-putting."

"Stupid bastard. I *knew* he was the problem in bed. Here's another guess. He's not into oral sex and the fact that you like it bothered him."

"How do you know I like it?" Keeping up with their conversation was becoming increasingly challenging while she fondled his hard-on.

"There's a lot to be said for enthusiasm and you're good at it." And it figured prominently in her fantasies. "You're a very open, giving lover." Unlike Helene. Sex had always been all about her. Hell, *everything* had always been all about her. "Your ex-husband was a moron."

She shrugged. "We just weren't compatible. This morning would've sent him over the edge."

"It sent *me* over the edge." In about two seconds she'd have him begging to go there again.

She worked his zipper down. "I like the way you go over the edge," she said, slipping her hand under the elastic of his briefs and freeing his cock. "Another half hour isn't going to make or break our schedule if you'd like to go again."

Cue the "Hallelujah Chorus." "There is nothing,

nothing I'd rather do. I was afraid that conversation with your mother might shut you down." Okay, so actually his mind must be shutting down because that was a dumb-ass thing to say right before…please God, he hoped he hadn't killed her mood.

"The damage is done," she said. She walked him backward until the back of his knees bumped against the couch's edge, her hand wrapped around his dick as if it were a navigational joystick. "I might as well be hung for a sheep as a lamb." She pushed lightly against his chest and he let himself fall back onto the couch.

"Is this where you want me?" he asked.

She settled on her knees in front of him, between his thighs. "That's right where I want you." She leaned forward and unbuckled his belt and released the button on his pants. "And this is just how I want you."

She wrapped her warm hand around his cock, stroking down and back up and…well, it felt good. She bent her head and he knew it was about to feel a whole lot better.

She teased her tongue along the length of his cock and then lapped at his head. Once. Twice. Three times a charm. Sam dropped his head to the back of the couch and moaned.

And then she took him in her hot, wet mouth…. "Oh, my God." He jerked his head upright.

She lifted her head and smiled. "Is that a *good* oh-my-god or a *bad* oh-my-god?"

"Good. Definitely good." And please do that again.

She smiled guilelessly. "It's those curiously strong

mints. I've always wanted to try them. I'm glad you like it."

She wrapped her lips over his shaft and took him into her mouth once again, her tongue stroking his cock, and the sensation roared through him again.

"No. I don't like it, I love it."

12

GISELLE SCRIBBLED the last of her notes as Sam eased them over the speed bump at the resort. The interviews with the Marches and the Watsons had gone extremely well.

"Finished?" he asked.

"For now. I'll work some of this into my article outline when I get back to the room." The late afternoon sun slanted through the SUV's window, picking out golden threads in Sam's dark brown hair. A ready smile bracketed his mouth and crinkled the corners of his eyes. She loved the way Sam's smile engaged his whole face. She also liked the way he frowned, furrowing lines across his forehead, when he was concentrating over his camera. She doubted he even realized he did it.

How could her sister have ever wanted another man when she'd had this one?

"If you've got more work and you don't mind, I need to run an errand," he said, pulling into a parking space.

"An errand?" He was running an errand? Damn. They had less than forty hours left before they got on an Atlanta-bound plane and he wanted to run an errand?

Make that a double damn. And obviously he wasn't quite as ready to jump her as she was to jump him.

More than once he'd looked at her this afternoon as if he couldn't wait to get her back to the cottage. *She'd* translated that gleam in his eyes as sexual promise. Good grief, he'd had her so wound up she'd caught herself daydreaming about her, Sam and her favorite vibrator while she was between interviews.

Not that Sam wasn't adequate. He was more than adequate, but it would be…interesting. And she'd never mentioned it to any of her previous partners because she suspected most men would feel it impugned their sexuality, but she thought it'd be hot. And she could've sworn Sam was in the same state she was because he'd been sporting a fairly distinctive bulge—not that she'd been crotch-watching or anything.

She'd had to concentrate damn hard on her notes during the drive back because *she'd* thought the air had fairly crackled with sexual tension between them.

Apparently, *she'd* been wrong if he was dropping her off and going back out to run a flaming errand. "Sure. Fine. No problem."

"I'll be back in about an hour and a half."

Okay. Apparently he was tired of her already. Certainly not very flattering. She got out of the vehicle and looked back at him, her hand on the door, ready to slam…er, close it.

"Don't rush back on my account. I've got a ton of work to do integrating my notes into my outline. In fact, as long as you're ready at the car by nine-thirty in the morning so we have time to get to the ten o'clock appointment—"

He held up a broad hand. "Giselle, I think you've got the wrong idea, honey."

No. Considering it was prime happy-hour time, he was probably meeting someone for drinks. Maybe that gorgeous red head behind the lobby desk of the Watson's hotel. She'd certainly been doing her darndest to chat Sam up. "You've obviously made plans—"

"I hate to disappoint you but all my plans include you." He looked her down…and then back up…as if she were undressed and he was touching her. It wasn't a look that worked when it came from a stranger, but from your lover, it worked in spades.

"Oh."

"I want to pick up a surprise for you."

"You don't have to get me anything."

"I *want* to get you something. I fully intend to get you something. I'm just not sure how long it'll take me to find it." Another up-and-down sweep of his hooded blue eyes and she was clinging to the car door for support. "What do you think about ordering room service tonight and eating in front of the fire?"

What do you think about me screwing your brains out? "That would be lovely."

"No." He shook his head. "*That* would be good. Lovely would be you naked in the firelight."

They really thought quite a bit alike.

"Hurry," she said, closing the door. Rather than stand around like a ninny watching him drive away, she headed for the stone path leading from the parking lot to the cottage.

She felt more as if she were floating rather than walking along the path. Surprises seldom came her way. What would Sam get her? She came to the cottage turnoff but suddenly waiting for Sam in the cottage didn't appeal. True enough, she had work to do, but when would she ever be in Sedona again? The Adirondack chair at the creek's edge beckoned. Why not?

She walked down the bank and settled into the chair. She rested her head against the slatted wood back and closed her eyes, absorbing the soothing rhythm of water flowing over rocks as the sun warmed her face. Time lost meaning as the swiftly-moving water lulled her into a tranquil state.

She drifted in and out of semi-consciousness. The murmur of water. The caress of the sun. Sam. It had always been Sam. It would always be Sam. She loved him. She had for a long time now. She always would. The thought settled over her like a warm, comforting blanket.

A child's strident tones jolted her back to full consciousness like a douse of cold water.

"But I want to play in the water!"

The mother grabbed the child's hand and towed him away from the stream as the kid launched into a fullfledged tantrum.

Giselle stood and stretched. So much for the peaceful creek.

"Sorry," the young mother called over her shoulder in Giselle's direction.

"No problem," she reassured her. She needed to get back to the room anyway and review her notes.

She headed back up the path to the cottage. She loved him. She loved Sam. In a way it was a relief to finally admit it to herself. She'd denied it. She'd run from it. She'd tried to hide behind physical attraction. She didn't fool herself that they had a future, but she did have the next two days.

FINDING A SHOP that catered to adult sex toys hadn't been as difficult as he'd thought. Actually, it'd been as simple as asking the resort's concierge, who hadn't blinked an eye as he provided name, address and location.

Sam perused the somewhat overwhelming array of vibrators in front of him. He knew there'd been one in that fantasy running through her head, but he had been so caught up in the action, he hadn't really paid close attention to the product itself. Pink? Purple? Ribbed? Silicone? Glass? Vibrating? Multiple speeds? Dammit. He wanted to get this right for her.

He paused. If luck was smiling on him, Giselle might indulge in that fantasy once again and this time he'd pay attention to the attendant vibrator. He paused, waiting. And waiting. And waiting some more. Nope. The amulet wasn't any warmer than usual against his skin and there was no precursor static playing in his head. Crap.

Just when he wanted his little nymphomaniac lover to drift off to fantasyland, she was obviously concentrating on something other than sex. It was probably a good thing. When he was watching them get it on in his head it was hard not to look like a pervert standing around with a hard-on. That, however, was a small price to pay for being privy to all her fantasies. He loved her sexual appetite, her lack of inhibition and her sexual sense of adventure.

He picked up a smooth, alabaster vibrator. Nah. Not a good choice for a woman who favored a red push-up bra and ho-ho-ho panties. He put it back on the shelf. A display shelf one down caught his eye. Now *that* looked just like something she'd like.

GISELLE HEARD Sam unlocking the cottage door but she resolutely continued incorporating her notes into her article outline. She was determined to enjoy her days… and nights…with him, but this time next week her brief affair with Sam would be history and she'd still need her job. Priorities.

He opened the door and stepped in, bringing a rush of frosty air with him. He quickly shouldered the door closed. Their gazes locked. Her heart thudded against her ribs and she looked away first, afraid she'd reveal what she'd just discovered for herself. Being stupid enough to fall in love with Sam was one thing, letting him know it was another altogether.

"I brought these for you," he said, setting a vase of fresh flowers on the corner of the desk, which just went to show that she was so scattered by his mere presence that she'd managed to overlook them.

Her ex-husband had never brought her flowers. Ever.

He was too cheap, although he couched his miserliness as practical—why spend money on something that was just going to die?

"Thank you. They're beautiful." And they were, even though she was basically too flower-ignorant to identify any of them. She still knew she liked being the recipient.

"They reminded me of you," he said.

Giselle looked at her laptop to hide the tears pricking at the back of her eyes. She would not ruin this by blubbering just because she found his words and the flowers achingly romantic.

"Almost through?" Sam asked, nuzzling the back of her neck and sending shivers through her. He wrapped his arms around her from behind, his hands stopping just below her breasts. "Miss me?"

"Hmm." Instinctively she moved to put her breasts into his hands. With a soft laugh he cupped them, bouncing them gently against his palms. He circled each nipple through her sweater and bra with his thumb.

"Give me two more minutes," she said in a breathless rush. "I hate to stop without finishing. Sometimes I lose my train of thought." She had a tenuous hold on it at best with his warm breath stirring the small hair on her nape and his talented hands on her tits.

He straightened. "I'll light the fire."

She glanced at him over her shoulder. "You just did."

"Baby, if you need to finish what you're doing, you better turn around and do it now. I've got plans."

"Promises, promises," she muttered teasingly as she

turned back to the keyboard. Who was she kidding? Her train of thought had derailed the moment Sam walked through the door. Nonetheless, she made a valiant effort to redirect her attention back to her work.

Effort was the definitive word. Concentrating on anything else proved impossible. To her right, he leaned down, checked that the fireplace flue was open and struck a match to the kindling. The fire caught.

Giselle looked back at the keyboard. Where was she in her notes? The fire crackled in the fireplace and aromatic juniper mingled with the flowers' perfume and Sam's scent.

Even though he was quiet, she heard him moving about. She knew he was there and the knowing superseded everything else.

What the heck? She was still staring at the same sentence she'd been staring at a few minutes ago. She tossed in the towel and stood.

"Finished?" Sam asked.

He sat on the couch, facing the fireplace. The coffee table held an open bottle of wine, two glasses and candles.

"I'm finished for now. I've been distracted."

"Good." His grin was almost boyish. "I was afraid I was the only one." He sobered, his eyes darkening. "Come here."

She paused for a second, committing to memory the scene before her. It was going to have to see her through a lifetime without him. Beneath the sexual arousal pulsing between them, a calm pervaded her, a rightness.

She crossed to him and started to sit next to him. He tugged her down onto his waiting lap instead.

He was warm and solid beneath her, some parts more solid than others. She wound her arms around his neck as he bent his head and kissed her. Teasing, short kisses gave way to longer, more intense exploration. Somewhere in the back of her mind the thought drifted by that she could easily spend the rest of her life right here, in his arms, kissing him.

Several kisses later, Giselle wound up on her back with Sam sprawled on top of her. Along the way she'd lost her sweater and he'd lost his shirt. He hooked one finger beneath her bra strap and tugged it aside. He levered himself up until he could look down at her and then he tugged harder, pulling the bra down to the point where her breast and nipple were exposed. He exhaled.

He wrapped his hand around her breast and she shivered beneath his touch.

"I can't seem to get enough of you." His voice was husky, low, aroused. He feathered his fingers up her chest to cup her jaw in his hand, his blue eyes holding her captive. "No other woman has ever looked, tasted or felt as good as you."

Reality reigned in that moment and she looked away from him into the dancing flames. "I know what I look like."

He gently forced her attention back to him. "Are you calling me a liar?"

"No, but, I—"

"You're incomparable. *No other woman*," he spoke slowly, with deliberate emphasis, "compares to you."

She got it. Without naming names, in a tasteful manner he'd just allayed one of her biggest insecurities. It was as if she'd just shed a lifetime of shackles. She pushed him up and crawled onto his lap, straddling him.

"Thank you for that," she said, reaching behind her to unhook her bra. She tossed it over the back of the couch.

He wrapped his hands around her waist and pulled her up, his tongue teasing first one ripe point and then the other. "It's the truth."

Several minutes later, they'd managed to divest themselves of all their clothes. Sam used his hands and mouth to pay homage to her in a most satisfactory manner.

He lifted his head. "Babe?"

"Yeah?"

"I bought something else for you…well, for us… while I was out today." His voice was as unsteady as she felt.

"Yes?" Running on pure arousal, she was beyond nervousness.

He leaned over and reached beneath the couch. "I brought something for you, but if it makes you uncomfortable, tell me."

She knew her eyes widened when he pulled out a molded plastic gift box with a purple ribbed vibrator with a curved tip. Finally! A man who was comfortable enough with his own penis to bring in back up. Oh, the things they could do with that.

"No. It doesn't make me uncomfortable at all," she said, unwrapping the vibrator. She'd just been thinking about this very thing earlier today. Sam had shown up yesterday morning and they'd wound up in the shower. It had played out very similarly to the way she'd fantasized, except it'd just been the two of them. It couldn't just be coincidence. Having someone so tuned in to her was a little freaky.

Sam pressed a hot, openmouthed kiss to her shoulder, bringing her back to the present and the burning need inside her.

"In fact, it makes me very, very hot." She arched her back and rubbed her pebbled nipples against his chest. "Not to mention dripping wet."

AN HOUR or so—and a helluva good time—later, Sam watched firelight shadows dance across Giselle's nakedness as they lay stretched out on the comforter he'd spread on the floor before the fireplace.

"I've got something to tell you that's going to sound pretty strange, but I want you to hear me out with an open mind," he said. He hadn't really planned to tell her now, but it just seemed as if he should.

She tucked her hair behind one ear, her expression wary. "Okay."

He recounted meeting Lisle and her giving him the amulet.

She traced her finger along the stone's edge where it lay against his skin, her touch sending tremors through him. "So this is supposed to bring you clarity? Has it?"

"Maybe. Hell, I don't know." He caught her hand in his, threading his fingers through hers. "The other part of this is that the clarity comes from someone else."

"In what way?"

"She told me it would be reflected through the fantasies of my lover."

"I don't get it."

"Think of it as an erotic telecommunicator. The fantasies sort of play out in my head like on a monitor or a TV screen."

A small frown wrinkled her forehead and she tightened her fingers around his. "So you want me to believe that you know women's fantasies when you're wearing that?"

"No. Not all women. She said it would only transmit the fantasies of the woman who awakened my inner desire. And my clarity would come through bringing her pleasure and fulfilling her needs." He pulled her to him. "It was you."

"Me? You've been tuning in to my fantasies?" She laughed. "Yeah, right." Her laughter faded and he could almost see the wheels turning as she quickly cataloged her fantasies and the sex they'd had. "You've been tuning in to my head!" She pushed away from him, betrayal and outrage in her eyes. "That's what this was all about? You're on some self-actualization quest? I'm so glad I could help." She looked torn between slapping him and crying, or maybe both.

Damn, he felt like a dog. And he was making a mess of explaining this to her. "No! A thousand times no. I don't know what all that clarity business is about. I just know that I've been tied up in knots from the first moment I saw you. I've never hungered for another woman the way I crave you. I knew we only had a few days here. I wasn't going to turn down *anything* that might get us together."

The rigid line of her shoulders softened. "I'm not sure whether I'm flattered that I awoke your inner desire or horrified that you've been reading my fantasies. Do you know everything I'm thinking?"

"No. Only your fantasies."

She rose and stood before the fireplace, silhouetted against the orange flames. "You had no right. That was private."

"I know I shouldn't have…but once I had it on, once I started tuning in to them…." He petered off. His excuse sounded lame even to him.

She closed her eyes momentarily and rubbed her fingers over her forehead. She looked away from him to the fire. "This is embarrassing."

"Baby, don't be embarrassed for a second. It's hot." He picked up the vibrator they'd discarded at the comforter's edge. Her intimate scent still clung to it. "Tell me this wasn't hot."

He let the memory fill the space between them. They'd both been on fire and it had driven her wild, which had driven him wild. He laid it back down on the comforter.

She licked her lips, "It was, but—"

He grasped the amulet. "Do you want me to take it off? Say the word and it's off."

"Do you want to take it off?"

"Only if you want me to. I meant what I said the other night. I want to give you what you want, how you want it, when you want it. I admit I like the inside track this gives me. I wouldn't have thought of that," he nodded toward the vibrator, "but it was beyond good."

"Fantasies only?"

"So far. Erotic telecommunication."

"That shower fantasy, three of us, you know I don't really want to—"

"If you told me you really wanted another guy, I'd try to wrap my head around that reality. Your fantasy excited me but I'm not sure I could actually handle another guy with you. While I was there, I mean." Not strictly true. The idea of another guy with her at all didn't work for him. "Speaking of other guys—" the lousy bastards could all drop dead "—when I saw your fantasies, I was the guy in there but the woman at the shop told me it could just be me projecting myself."

Screw it if he sounded kind of needy and insecure; he wanted to know.

She knelt at the comforter's edge. "You weren't projecting. It was you." She raised her chin, firelight picking out the gleam of challenge in her hazel eyes. "Now let's see if you play fair, Sam. You've been peeking at every sexual fantasy I've had in the last twenty-four hours, so why don't you tell me one of yours."

He squirmed. "I don't know, babe. I don't really fantasize. I'm curious about things but not real imaginative. I don't have the imagination you do…although I definitely appreciate yours." He grinned.

"Thanks for making me feel like a deviant freak." Her smile belied her words. "You told me you'd imagined me naked before." She traced her finger from his hip to his navel. "When? Why?"

"Honey, I've thought about you naked so many times in the past two years that the *when* is mind-boggling." He grinned. "And the *why* should be obvious."

She circled the circumference of his belly button, her nail scraping deliciously against him. "In the car on the way from the airport," he said. "I got this instant shot of the two of us in bed together."

"What were we doing?" She dragged her fingernail from his navel to the edge of his pubic hair.

Sam sucked in a breath. *Lower, lower.* "My cock was buried inside you and I was stroking your clit."

"Oh." Avoiding his growing cock, she moved her finger lower to stroke his inner thigh. She was driving him insane. Two could play at that game.

"And I wondered what your breasts were like." He circled her areola with his fingertip. "What color your nipples were." He smoothed his palm over the turgid point and then caught it between his thumb and forefinger, squeezing gently. "What size." He slid his hand down over her belly to cup her sex. "And whether you were a waxer or au naturel. Where your freckles stopped. And that's the difference between curiosity and imagination. I wondered but I wasn't very good at filling in the blanks." He found her clit with his finger, and she lifted her hips against him. "But the blanks are filled in very, very nicely. Better than nice."

She wrapped her hand around his cock—hallelujah. "You're much better in the flesh than in my imagination."

"My flesh is very happy to be here," he said, "and I love your imagination, except for that cowboy last night." She was wet against his hand. And he still wasn't sure if she'd been fantasizing about him or Cowboy Luke. And hell, yeah, he was jealous.

"You didn't recognize the cowboy?"

"The part I saw was only from the back. The cowboy hat, chaps, and bare ass didn't ring a bell." His throat went dry as her fingers did something yummy against his penis.

"It was you. Sorry I got the derriere wrong. I was still working off imagination. And once again, you've proved better in the flesh."

His flesh was supremely happy to be with her flesh at the moment. And damn glad he was starring front and center for her rather than Cowboy Luke or Jimbob or whatever the hell his name had been. "Me? Really? Too bad I didn't pick up a bale of hay, a cowboy hat and some leather chaps."

"Hey, sometimes you've just got to improvise." She rolled to her hands and knees and issued an invitation in an over-the-shoulder-glance. "You have the bare ass and, well, that's really the only necessary prop, isn't it? A bare ass is a terrible thing to waste."

He laughed as he clambered to his knees, almost clumsy in his haste and, he realized, relief. In that second he acknowledged just how damn scared he'd been that when he told her the truth about the amulet he'd never have the chance to make love to her again. And on that point he'd gained total clarity—not making love to her again didn't work for him at all.

13

TWO DAYS LATER, on Christmas Eve, Giselle shivered as Sam settled into the center seat on the airplane beside her. Within a few minutes, they'd taxied down the runway and were on their way. They'd both been quiet on the trip back to Phoenix, moved and awed by the early morning ceremony at the vortex.

She'd wondered if it wouldn't be a bit of a three-ring circus with eight couples showing up—as well as White Dove, and a dozen assorted singles plus her and Sam. Far form being a circus, everyone was reverent, giving a quiet spiritualism to the whole event. And if she'd ever doubted before, she believed now. The energy had been a powerful force, moving through her, in her, markedly stronger than the day before when she and Sam has scouted out the site.

She couldn't wait to see Sam's photographs. Had he captured the sheer radiance of the morning? The sun glinting off the red rocks? The golden shimmer that seemed to dance on the air around those present? But it would be up to her to tell the reader of the emotions, the love that permeated her, that seemed to intensify with every heartbeat. She'd sworn she wouldn't show up there with Sam, but the damage was already done. She had, however, kept herself busy with notes and taking in the ceremony. And she was stubbornly clinging to this experience with Sam until the very last minute when they disembarked in Atlanta. Three hours to go.

She stifled a yawn.

"Tired?" Sam asked.

"Maybe a little."

"That's what happens when you keep me up all night."

"I didn't hear any complaints earlier," she said, teasing him in return.

He pushed the armrest between them up and out of the way. "Here, lean against me." He unfolded the blanket and tucked it around her. The tenderness and gentleness in his action were nearly her undoing.

She settled against him, loving his solid warmth, desperate to touch him as closely as she could while she still could. Heck, if she could climb up on his lap without raising eyebrows she would.

Exhaustion weighed her eyes and she drifted into that no-man's-land between sleep and full wakefulness. Fantasy stole in. She and Sam on the blanket in front of the fire, his fullness in her mouth, the vibrator in her—

"Giselle," Sam said, snapping her into wakefulness. "You're killing me, baby. We're on a plane. It's not nearly as easy for me to walk after you've been thinking about that as it is for you."

She laughed. "Oops. I guess not." She grew serious. "I think it's time for you to take the amulet off, Sam."

He tightened his arm around her shoulders, pulling her into him closer still. "Just a little longer. I will when we get to Atlanta."

She nodded. "When we get to Atlanta. And you have to promise you won't put it back on."

"No. Once I take it off, you have my word I won't put it back on. That way lies madness. It would make me crazy to wonder if it was me in your fantasies or simply me putting myself there. I don't particularly want to know when your inner desire shifts to someone else."

He caressed her temple with a phantom brush of his lips. "I was thinking…I could call you next week and maybe we could meet for coffee or lunch. We could go over the article and the photographs."

They'd steadfastly avoided talking about life past Sedona. She clamped down on the joy that welled inside her. Coffee. Lunch. Let's be friends. Giselle, the girl everyone wanted for a friend. Could she stand to see Sam starting a relationship with someone else? No. There was no future with Sam. She'd known it before she slept with him. What the hell? She'd known it two years ago. How many times did it take for her to learn the same lesson?

"No. Don't call me. You can send Monica the photos. Or I'm sure she would love to meet you for lunch."

He pulled back as if she'd struck him. "I'll courier them to her. I'm not interested in meeting her for lunch, or anything else."

"Fine."

"Fine."

The plane hadn't even landed and already things were strained and weird.

DESPERATION CHURNED in his gut as Sam rode the steep escalator to Atlanta's Hartsfield-Jackson baggage claim area behind Giselle. Ten minutes, twenty tops if the baggage handlers were slow unloading the plane, and she was going to gather her luggage and leave. She'd already made it clear the assignment was over and that meant they were over. He didn't want her to walk out of his life.

They streamed off the escalator with the other passengers and took a left to the baggage claim.

"Our luggage should be at carousel three," Giselle said. He followed her silently because he wasn't so damn sure that if he opened his mouth he wouldn't beg her not to walk out of his life. And Sam had never begged for anything or anyone.

What the hell? He hadn't felt this sense of having been kicked in the balls the night he'd found Helene and Danny in bed or the day his final divorce papers had arrived. But then he'd never loved Helene the way he loved Giselle.

He swayed as if he'd been broadsided with a two-by-four.

"Are you okay, Sam?" Giselle asked, concern furrowing her brow, softening her features.

"I'm fine." Damn, he felt as if he couldn't breathe.

He was thinking with his dick. He wanted her. He'd always wanted her, but he didn't love Giselle Randolph. He didn't know how to love someone. That was…sweet Jesus…he loved her.

"I love you," he blurted out.

"What?" She stared at him as if he'd lost his mind. He was pretty damn sure he had…right along with his heart. She'd stolen both.

Not only was she staring at him, the people immediately around them were staring, as well. *Have some balls, man.* "I said, I love you."

She shot him a tight smile. "No, you don't."

"Yes, I do."

"You do not." She crossed her arms over her chest. "It's the sex talking."

A teenage boy snickered and his girlfriend elbowed him. "Excuse us." Sam grabbed Giselle's elbow and dragged her over to a more private spot—well, as private as you could get at one of the busiest airports in the country on Christmas Eve night. "It is the best sex I've ever had but it is not the sex talking."

"You aren't—"

He cut her off. Being in love had him on edge. "Don't tell me how I do or don't feel, dammit." He ran his hand through his hair, searching for the right words. He didn't find them soon enough.

"Sam, just because we had great sex together doesn't translate to love." Her hollow laugh lacked amusement. "We've both known this was impossible anyway. Have you forgotten you were married to my sister? I haven't.

Do you really think for a minute anyone would believe this wasn't a subconscious desire to get back at her? Showing up with the short end of the stick? And don't you think it's going to be a little awkward sitting at the dinner table? You, me, Helene and Danny? How does that play out? There's not exactly any love lost between the three of you."

He caught her chin in his hand, tilting her face up to his, and looked in her eyes. Dammit, she was running again. "I don't know what it is that you're so afraid of, honey, but you know this thing between you and me…" he shook his head. "It's been there since your 'Mr. Wonderful, I presume.' You know this isn't about getting back at her. The only thing that's ever been about Helene is when I met you and knew I'd married the wrong sister."

She winced and bowed her head, as if she needed a second to gather her composure. She looked up, nodding. "You're right. And I know it and you know it, but the rest of the world—"

"Doesn't matter." He captured her hands and held them in his. "And never, ever refer to yourself as the short end of the stick. You're twice the woman Helene is." He felt her tension, saw her bristle. "I know she's your sister and I know she's the baby and your entire family has spoiled her damn rotten, but the truth is the truth and you're going to hear it. You are twice the woman she is, in every regard, every respect."

She was listening, but he didn't think she was hearing. He wasn't sure he was getting through to her.

"Look, I know why Helene slept with Danny. I didn't love her. Ever since I was a kid, I was determined to have the best, to show the world Sam McKendrick was worthy. Worthy of what I don't exactly know…crap, I'm doing a lousy job of explaining myself. Anyway, I'm not proud of it but Helene was more of an accessory than a wife. She looked good. She fit into my plan, but everything was superficial between us. She never touched me inside the way you do. I don't know if that was because I didn't let her or because we just didn't have between us what I think you and I have between us. Clarity. I've never seen myself so clearly my entire life. I don't need this anymore." He took off the amulet. "And you asked me to take it off when we arrived anyway." He dropped it into his pocket.

"Sam, I'm truly happy that you figured out what went wrong between you and Helene. You gained insight into yourself and that's fantastic, but don't make this out to be something between us that's simply not there. A week from now, possibly a month from now, you'll figure it out and then I'll be left with a disaster because my having a relationship with you will wreck my family. You'll move on and I'll just be part of the wreckage left behind."

"Why are you so sure I'll move on? I love you, Giselle. I'm not a young boy or even a young man any more. I've never felt this way about anyone before and I know in my soul I never will."

"You don't even really know me."

"Babe, do you think Helene never mentioned you?

As you keep pointing out, I *was* married to her. There was a picture of you two that sat on our dresser every day for the time we were together."

She shook her head in silent denial. She walked over to the luggage carousel. Their bags were the last two making the trip round and round. She plucked her yellow suitcase off.

"If you'll send the pictures to Monica, she'll take care of things."

Her back remained ramrod straight as she walked out into the night, her suitcase in tow. Somehow, some way he'd convince her.

He realized she'd thrown every roadblock in the book his way, but nowhere along the way had she said she didn't love him and that was all that really mattered. However, winning her over to the idea of *them* was going to take some doing.

Sam could use a miracle…or two.

GISELLE PULLED into her parents' driveway, parking her Bug behind Helene and Danny's Saab. A lamp glowed softly in the front window, welcoming her home. Her mom would've left that for her. Mom never left the house dark when one of her girls was due to arrive. Hot tears pricked the back of her eyelids at the comforting familiarity of the Christmas lawn ornaments and the glowing lamp when so much of her felt at odds with the norm.

And dammit, what about Sam? What was he coming home to? A dark, empty house? Did he even have a Christmas tree? He'd told her he loved her—in the baggage claim area, no less. The mere thought weakened her knees, battered her resolve. She couldn't, wouldn't allow herself to believe it. Like a mantra learned over a lifetime, she repeated the words to herself: men like Sam didn't fall in love with women like her. Men like Sam fell in love with women like Helene. And if for a fleeting moment of fantasy she allowed herself to believe he loved her, that they stood a chance, how could she possibly leave him to face this first Christmas alone without his mother? But how could she walk away from her family to be with him? How could she bring him home with her?

Exhaustion and hopelessness rooted her to the car seat. She rested her weary head on the steering wheel. What the heck should she do? What did she want? Did she want Sam at the expense of her family? Did Sam have to come at the expense of her family? Oh, for a little of that clarity he'd found in Sedona. She'd gone there for healing and, if anything, she felt more battered and confused than before.

A light tap sounded at her car window. She looked up. Her mother, her robe knotted at her waist, stood outlined by the streetlamp.

Giselle unlocked the door and climbed out.

"What're you doing out here this late, Mom?"

"I heard you drive up. You didn't come in so I came to get you. I thought you might need some help."

Giselle dragged out a smile. "Just tired. It's been a long day." She opened the back door and hoisted out her bag. "Let's get inside. You must be freezing."

"It's a bit chilly out." Her mother ushered her forward with a guiding hand to her elbow, as if she hadn't traversed this driveway hundreds, no thousands, of times before as a kid and a teenager.

"Everyone else asleep?" Giselle asked as the front door snicked in place behind them.

"Yes. Of course I couldn't sleep until you got home. It's always been that way when I was expecting one of you girls. Come on into the kitchen and I'll fix you a drink." She paused. "I left the tree lights on for you."

"Thanks, Mom." Giselle found little joy but great comfort in the tree trimmed with a lifetime of memories in the corner of the den. Greenery lined the mantel, all of their stockings hung in a neat row. The familiarity of Randolph family Christmas soothed her in a way nothing else could. She slipped off her shoes in the foyer and trudged barefoot down the hall behind her mother.

Her absolute favorite part of the kitchen renovation from a year ago was the addition of the "keeping room" adjacent to the kitchen. Two overstuffed armchairs upholstered in a cream and black toile and a red camelback love seat invited guest to relax and enjoy the company of the cook while she, or occasionally he, performed culinary magic. Giselle all but collapsed into one of the armchairs.

"Vanilla or rum?" her mom asked as she pulled out a saucepan.

"Rum." Mom's idea of a near-midnight drink had always been warm milk with a pinch of sugar and a dash of vanilla. Once her girls were in college, she'd given them the option of rum rather than vanilla.

"The bench was delivered today. It's beautiful. Daddy was tickled pink."

They exchanged desultory conversation while her mother warmed the milk over a low gas flame. Quiet descended with only the occasional attendant creak and groan that came with old houses. Her mother split the steaming liquid between two Spode Christmas mugs and added a healthy splash of rum to each. She passed one to Giselle and settled in the chair opposite her.

"You look terrible."

"Gee, thanks, Mom." It was true. She'd had very little sleep the past nights and she was pretty damn miserable to boot, but for some reason hearing it from her mother hurt her feelings.

Her mother's mouth pinched. "It's Sam, isn't it? I've been worried sick ever since I knew he was there with you."

"I just feel bad for him that he's alone at Christmas. I came home to this, he's going home to nothing."

"Why doesn't he go home to that whore he slept with while he was married to your sister?"

"Then it could be a trend since my sister's with the whore she was sleeping with when she was married to Sam," Giselle snapped, frustration and exhaustion outweighing good judgment and discretion.

"What did you say?" Her mother blanched.

"Nothing. I don't even know what I said. I'm just tired. I think I'll take my milk to my room," she said, rising to her feet.

"No, ma'am, you won't. You'll sit back down and tell me what you meant by that."

Treads squeaked in the front of the house. Giselle sank back to her seat. "Mom, I—"

Helene walked into the kitchen, pushing her long blond hair out of her eyes. "I thought I heard voices. I had to come down to wish my big sister a Merry Christmas now that she's finally shown up."

"You come sit down," her mother said. "I believe you've got some explaining to do."

14

"WHAT'S GOING ON? Is everything okay?" Helene asked, perching on the edge of the love seat, a smudge of old mascara beneath one eye.

Their mother cut straight to the chase. She was good at that. "Sam was Giselle's photographer on her Sedona assignment."

"*My* Sam? My Sam was there with you when I talked to you? You shared a cabin with him?" Outrage flared in Helene's eyes, but there was also a hint of panic.

"A cottage," Giselle said. "It was actually a cottage." She lifted her chin, "And he's not *your* Sam anymore." She spoke softly but she might as well have shouted.

"Oh. My. God. You slept with him. I can see it all over your face. How could you?" Her sister's nostrils flared with accusation. "I should've known he would do whatever he could to get back at me."

Giselle had practically said the same thing to Sam earlier, but it hurt hearing it from Helene—the implication that revenge would be the only motive in his sleeping with her, as if real attraction couldn't possibly be a factor.

Even though she was still angry with Helene for her deception and she was none too happy about her comment, Giselle silently urged her sister to step up to the plate and come clean. "You told us all you got a divorce because he was unfaithful. Why would he get back at you for that?"

"I don't know what you're talking about."

"Lena…" Giselle lapsed into the childhood nickname, the name from days when they sat under a makeshift tent in the parlor and played with Barbie dolls and engaged in endless rounds of Candy Land that Giselle always let her baby sister win.

Helene twisted her long, elegant fingers and shame crumpled her features as she looked away from both of them. "Because I was having an affair with Danny while we were married."

Their mother shrank back into her chair. "Oh, Helene."

"I'm sorry, Mama." Tears sparkled in Helene's eyes. "I know it was wrong. And it was wrong for me to let everyone think it was all Sam's fault, but everyone loved Sam and I was afraid the family wouldn't accept Danny if you knew the truth." Her voice cracked. "And I didn't want to see you look at me the way you're looking at me now."

"You know I'm going to love you no matter what, but I'm disappointed."

Helene's face took on a tight, petulant look at their mother's censure. It was as if they were five and seven again, or make it fifteen and seventeen and Helene was complaining that Giselle never got in trouble. "Are you disappointed in Giselle? She slept with my ex-husband. Do you have any idea what it's like to live with a man when you realize he doesn't love you? And when another man tells you he's loved you from the first minute he ever saw you? I swear, we never meant for it to happen, but once it did, neither of us was strong enough to walk away. We were going to tell Sam. We were waiting for the right time but the right time never came. And then he came home early from a trip and we both knew it was over. I kept waiting for him to tell you and Daddy. Danny and I both waited and waited and then he didn't and we thought it was just best to let it all go away and get on with life. I think we've both known this day would come sooner or later." She glared at Giselle. "But I really never thought it would come because my sister screwed my ex-husband."

"Watch your mouth, young lady," her mother snapped. Isobel Randolph didn't tolerate any hint of vulgarity.

Stark jealousy shone in Helene's eyes along with accusation. "You've wanted him for a long time, haven't you, Giselle? Two years ago, Christmas night," she taunted "Tell me you didn't want him."

Sam had been absolutely right. Helene had been jealous. Apprehension and guilt knotted Giselle's gut. However, she raised her chin, anger lending her an edge of defiance. "Yes, I wanted him." Her mother's gasp echoed in the room. "The difference between you and me is that I took myself as far from temptation as possible." Which wasn't exactly a fair analogy because if Sam had actually made a move, she wasn't too darn sure how much strength she'd have had to turn him down. She'd like to think, however, that she would never have betrayed her sister with her husband. Post-divorce had been another matter.

Helene bristled. Their mother looked equally stunned and confused, with some added disbelief for good measure.

"There was something going on between you and Sam two years ago?" her mother asked.

"No. Not really. I developed a crush on him, that's all."

The look on Helene's face wasn't pretty. "Well, how was it after two years, sis? Didn't you wonder if he was thinking about me?"

Giselle recoiled as if she'd been struck. Her sister had sliced to the heart of Giselle's insecurity.

Their mother stood, regal and commanding, even in a bathrobe, her mouth tight with displeasure. "Enough. You won't speak to your sister that way. We're all tired and we're going to bed now. We'll sort this out in the morning."

Giselle squared her shoulders, ignoring the daggers Helene sent her way, and walked out of the kitchen ahead of her mother and her sister. She was exhausted, true enough, but she didn't really see how any of this would be any better tomorrow morning. This was a steaming, stinking pile of mess.

As she started up the stairs, the grandfather clock in the hall began its stentorian chiming, signaling midnight.

Merry Christmas.

SAM ROLLED OUT of bed and wandered to the window that overlooked the Atlanta skyline. Eight o'clock in the morning and he hadn't slept yet. Bleakness etched his soul. He turned away from the window and headed down the hall to the den.

He poured himself a measure of the single malt scotch he'd gotten as a Christmas gift from a client a year ago. He tossed it back and winced as it burned all the way down. Nasty stuff, but wasn't that what the poor son of a bitch in the movies did when he felt as if a woman had ripped out his heart just about the time he figured out he had one?

Sam wasn't naive enough to expect a cure, he just wanted to anesthetize himself against the pain. He missed Giselle like…dammit, why couldn't he ever come up with any of those good metaphor things…he missed her like shit. That's how much he missed her. Even if she'd broken his heart, stomped on it and handed it right back to him.

He wanted to see her. He'd promised her he would take the amulet off and wouldn't put it back on. Wait, had he actually promised? His brain mangled the exact details, but what the hell? If he put the amulet on, he'd at least see her in his head and he was that sorely desperate.

He didn't care that he was pathetic. The amulet was in his pocket in his bedroom. What was she going to do, dump him for putting it back on? Too late. She'd already dumped him. Maybe he'd find some clarity to figure out how the hell to fix things. At the least he'd see her. Naked, too, since it worked in fantasy mode.

He retrieved his jeans from where he'd thrown them over the edge of the dresser. He shoved his hand down into his right pocket. No amulet. He felt harder. What the…there was a hole. He nearly howled in frustration. Dammit. He'd never had a hole in his pocket before and now he'd lost the magic amulet.

Yeah, that's right. Magic. He'd never believed in magic before. Of course, he'd never been in love before, either. Which had come first, the magic or the love? And how the hell was he supposed to work that out right now? He threw his pants with the holey pocket across the room and stalked back into the den.

This time he skipped the civility of a glass and swigged directly from the upended scotch bottle. Who gave a flying duck about civility? He was a caveman without his mate. What would a caveman do? A caveman would go and claim what was his. Giselle was his. The woman, his woman, had some crazy notions and some even crazier insecurities, but it seemed to him that love was blind to all of that—he was navigating uncharted waters here—and they'd just have to work through them. Because he was dead-ass certain she loved him. They'd waited two long years to find out if their chemistry was real. Not only was it real, but what they had was so much more than just chemistry. And he'd stood with her at the vortex on Love Day. If, after all of that, she thought she could just walk away, she had another thing coming. Namely him. For her.

So what if it meant facing his ex-wife, his ex-best friend, his former in-laws and the woman who told him she didn't want him on Christmas Day on their turf? A man had to do what a man had to do.

He eyed the Scotch bottle and debated another swallow of Dutch courage. Nah. Better not. He needed his wits about him and this was going to be awkward enough without him showing up half-sloshed. He headed back to his bedroom to get dressed. It'd probably go better if he didn't show up naked.

"DID SOMEONE die and no one wants to tell me about it?" Ford Randolph asked as the last present was unwrapped Christmas morning.

Helene promptly burst into tears. Danny put his arm around his wife, squirming on the sofa. To each his own that Helene had forsaken Sam for this man, Giselle thought. Whatever.

Their mother sighed but sat up straighter. "Well, dear, I thought we might make it through the day without addressing this, but it does in fact feel as if someone has died but it's not so straightforward. It seems that Danny and Helene were carrying on an affair, which is actually why Sam had a retaliatory one-night stand. And then the boat got rocked when Sam wound up going to Sedona as Giselle's photographer this past week and they had a bit of a fling because apparently they've had a thing for each other for the past two years." She ran out of breath and story at the same time.

"That's all old news, Isobel," their father said, waving a dismissing hand. "Well, except for the part about Giselle and Sam this week. And that took long enough."

Daddy *knew*? Giselle gaped, along with Danny and her mother. Helene stopped crying. Their mother recovered her wits first. "What are you talking about, Ford? Did you get into the Christmas brandy early?"

"For Pete's sake woman, haven't you had a clue what's been going on around us? Danny and Helene get married three months after the divorce and he constantly looks as if he expects momentary castration. I knew Sam had been cuckolded."

Danny flinched and kept his mouth shut. Probably the best tactic when your wife's father has just mentioned your name in conjunction with castration.

"But you never said anything," her mother accused.

He shrugged. "I figured constantly waiting for the other shoe to drop was fitting punishment. And as for Giselle and Sam, it was apparent two years ago they were half in love with each other, but they had to work things out in their own time and space. And well, he was married to Helene at the time."

Giselle found her voice. "Daddy, I'm sure you're wrong that he was half in love with me—"

He cut her off. "Was I wrong about Danny and Helene?"

"Well, no."

Helene blew her nose. "I'm sorry, Giselle, for what I said last night. I was way out of line. I was a bitch."

"It's all right," Giselle said automatically, and then she caught herself. Sam was right. They did all baby

Helene too much. Ultimately, they weren't doing her any favors. "Wait. You're right. You were a bitch." Helene's mouth dropped open. "I accept your apology."

Everyone waited to see how Helene would take the rebuke. Helene calling herself a bitch was one thing, Giselle repeating it, that was another.

Helene snapped her mouth shut, nodded, stood and held out her arms. "I'm sorry."

Giselle hugged her. "Thank you."

Helene clung to her. "I don't want you to hate me." Her voice wavered, as if she was one step away from crying again.

"I don't hate you," Giselle said, smoothing her hand over Helene's back the same way their mother had when they were small children. "We're sisters, remember?"

Helene's laugh still held a watery note.

Danny stood up, squaring his shoulders. "I owe this family an apology." He looked at their father. "I'm sorry, sir."

Ford nodded and stepped forward to shake Danny's hand. "Accepted."

"There's one more present under the tree," Helene said. Leave it to her little sister to notice, particularly if it redirected the attention from her and Danny. She wriggled beneath the tree—to the very back—and pulled out a square box wrapped in gold paper and a red bow. She looked at the attached card. "It's for you, Giselle," she said, passing it over.

A funny tingling swirled through Giselle. Her hands

weren't quite steady as she took the package. All eyes focused on her as she pulled off the bow, ripped the paper and lifted the lid.

All the air seemed to whoosh out of her body. Sam's amulet lay nestled in a bed of soft cotton batting.

"What is it?"

"Who's it from?"

Giselle ignored them all, lifted the amulet and fastened it around her neck despite her shaking hands. She waited, expecting a lightning bolt of clarity to strike her at any moment. Nothing. Nada.

"What is it, exactly?" her mother said.

Helene wrinkled her elegant nose. "It's kind of ugly, if you ask me."

No lightning bolts struck. No minitelevision turned on in her head. Instead, she could almost hear White Dove's soothing tone: "Caution is wise, fear is debilitating." Followed by Sam: "I don't know what you're so afraid of…"

Realization came. Not some huge epiphany that struck her over the head, but an understanding that blossomed from her heart.

She'd turned down Sam and walked away from him last night because she'd *wanted* to paint the situation impossible. She'd wanted the out. This was her family and she loved them. They would love her regardless. She and Sam as a couple. Danny and Helene. The road might be rocky and uncomfortable at times, but they'd navigate it.

No, it all came down to fear. She'd hidden behind

the insecurity blanket, but the truth of the matter was that what she felt for Sam scared the stuffing out of her. She'd known from the first moment that there was something powerful between them. Anything that instant, that powerful could decimate her. On an instinctive level she'd recognized Sam McKendrick was her Achilles heel. Her weak point. And she'd run, long and hard. And she'd been so damn determined and desperate to "cure" herself of Sam in Sedona. And once she'd admitted to herself that she loved him, she'd run from that too. She hadn't been afraid, she'd been *terrified* of just how much Sam meant to her. And the fact of the matter was she could run for forever and she would never "cure" herself of Sam McKendrick. This kind of love, what they had, didn't come with a safety outlet.

She fingered the amulet, finding an odd courage in the smooth, carved stone. She slowly looked around the room, making momentary eye contact with everyone. She opened her mouth to speak and sort of squeaked instead. She cleared her throat, stood straighter and tried again.

"I love Sam. I've loved Sam for a long time now. Sorry, Helene, but from the first moment I saw him." She felt as if she'd just taken the first step in a twelve-step recovery program.

"I knew it," Helene said, but there was no censure or rancor, rather an accepting weariness.

Giselle nodded an acknowledgement and continued speaking, eager to get it all out in the open now that she'd found her voice. "He told me last night that he loved me and I was too scared to handle it. He doesn't belong by himself today. I can't stand to think of him being alone. I love you all but I have to leave."

Her mother looked stricken. "But we've always spent Christmas Day together, ever since you were born, honey."

"There is one other option." She looked at her parents. It was, after all, their house. "We can all be together today."

"Oh, God. Do you know how uncomfortable that would be for me and Danny?" Helene blurted. Then she seemed to realize exactly what she'd said and how she'd said it. "But we'll manage. Not a problem. Really. It'll be fun. Just like old times."

"Honey, you might want to just quit now," their mother said in a gentle tone to Helene.

Giselle caught her sister up in a hug and laughed. "You're right, it's going to be weird and uncomfortable at first. I'm not sure I'd count on fun and I hope like hell—"

"Watch your mouth, young lady," her mother interjected.

"Sorry, Mom. I hope like heck it's *not* like old times, but we'll all be fine." She looked at her parents. Would she and Sam be welcome here? If not, the two of them would start their own Christmas tradition. From now on they were a package deal. "Mom? Dad?"

"I've missed Sam," her father said and Giselle *almost* felt sorry for Danny. "That boy can throw a mean game of horseshoes."

Giselle started. She'd had no idea.

Her mother paused, a moment that felt like forever, and then nodded, a smile lighting her eyes. "I'll set another place at the table. And you might want to let Sam know."

15

SAM CLOSED the kitchen door behind him with a distinct sense of déjà vu. The aroma of roasting turkey and spices mingled with the crisp scent of evergreens greeted him. The kitchen had been updated with granite countertops and new appliances, but the teakettle clock still hung on the wall and cookie makings littered the counter.

"I left him a message and I'm trying to stay busy so I don't go crazy until I hear from him." That familiar feminine voice was once again muffled as she rooted around in the corner cabinet, her very familiar, very delectable ass shoved up in the air. He'd have to remember to ask Isobel to never move that cookie sheet from that storage spot. It was just too delicious to watch Giselle wiggle her fanny around while locating it.

The same as two years ago, she backed out, stood up, saw him, and the cookie sheet clattered to the floor. Fast forward, new script, except Giselle Randolph was still a hot mess. And she was still the sexiest woman he'd ever seen. Bar none.

"I called your condo and left a message," she said, her eyes welcoming him.

"I heard." He motioned to the gaping cabinet door. "Just now."

She waved at the cookie dough and counter mess. "I was trying to keep busy until I heard from you." She pointed to her T-shirt. It was the I Brake For Elves and her red plunging bra under it. "I put this on for you."

"How'd you know I'd come?"

"A girl can always hope."

"That must've been some message you left."

She nodded. "I love you, Sam McKendrick."

"I know." He opened his arms and she took a flying leap into them, wrapping her arms around his neck and her legs around his waist. His mouth latched onto hers and he kissed her with all the passion and happiness and hunger that welled inside him. She offered the same.

Several minutes later, they untangled themselves from one another, and Giselle's eyes widened when she finally noticed his overnight bag slung over his shoulder.

"You came to stay?"

"I came prepared to do whatever I needed to do until I'd convinced you. I actually had some notion of being a caveman come to drag you off to my cave because you're mine."

"How primitive." Her smirk was frankly sensual. "I like it. My parents were…?"

"Out arguing over the light display," he finished.

"How was it?"

"The light display is great. Your parents? Damn awkward at first, but I think we're all okay now. They said Danny and Helene were off on a long walk."

Giselle smiled, a sly, sexy curve of her lips. "Come on. I'll show you to your room." She grabbed his hand and tugged him toward the hall, tossing a coy look over her shoulder. "You've got different accommodations this time."

They were halfway up the stairs when he stopped her. "Hold on a minute."

She turned, one stair above him, at eye level. He cupped her face in his hands, losing himself in the depths of her green-flecked eyes. He'd wanted to do this for so long. Two years had come and gone, and still something real and hot and dangerous pulsed between them. She swayed toward him. He leaned in. Their lips met.

Magic. Her kiss was pure magic.

They released one another and he followed her up the stairs, passing the second floor, on up to the attic, Giselle's space.

He ducked his head as he stepped through the doorway into a sloped-ceilinged area with an ensuite bathroom. Windows buttressed each end of the room, one overlooking the street, the other overlooking the rear garden. Both windows boasted cushioned window seats. Her bed, a wrought-iron affair with rumpled yellow sheets sat tucked beneath the sloping eave. A desk stood against the other eave, directly opposite the bed. The remaining wall belonged to overflowing bookcases. Cozy. Intimate. And it smelled like her.

Sam noticed the amulet around her neck. "Ah, you found it."

She fingered the carved stone. "I want to know how you wrapped it and got it under the Christmas tree."

Under the tree? "You didn't find it on the floor at the airport?"

"No. It was in a gift box under the tree this morning."

He shook his head. "You saw me put it in my pocket last night. When I checked this morning, there was a hole in my pocket and no amulet."

They shared a look. A look probably very similar to the one they'd shared after the truck spun them out with a sideswipe and there were no marks on the car. Cue *Twilight Zone* music. They'd both come to accept that sometimes the inexplicable happened.

She trailed her fingers over his chest, "You must be tired. Exhausted, probably. I think a little bed time, while the house is quiet and deserted, is just what you need."

He sank onto the edge of the sagging mattress and pulled her down in his lap. "I think that's just what I need."

Sam still didn't know what had brought about her change of heart, or rather her acknowledgement of her heart. He'd find out sooner or later. And it didn't really matter how she'd reached the realization she had. All that mattered was she loved him and they were together.

While he'd been reflecting, she'd been unbuttoning. She tugged his shirt off. With an indistinct murmur, she pressed an openmouthed, sucking kiss to his shoulder while her fingers continued a southbound exploration. She dipped her head and swirled her tongue around his nipple. He couldn't think when she was doing that.

She tugged her shirt over her head, revealing that ball-tightening red bra showcasing her splendid breasts. "Are you going to be able to handle this with my family? Danny's not going away, and Helene is my sister and I love her."

He swallowed hard before answering, amazed he could still string a coherent sentence together when she reached behind her to unsnap her bra. "I know it's going to be a little awkward, especially at first, but I would walk across burning coals for you. I can sit down to dinner with Helene and Danny. In fact, I should thank them. Otherwise Helene and I might still be dragging along unhappily together."

She tossed her bra to the floor and leaned forward to rub her breasts in lazy, erotic circles over his chest. "It's probably best not to get too carried away."

He bent his head and tugged her nipple into his mouth, sucking. Her hiss of indrawn breath told him she was beginning to lose the conversational thread also. He let her go.

She shimmied out of her pants and panties while he kicked off his jeans and briefs. She pushed him onto his back on the mattress and stretched out beside him. "With the folks outside, as the stand-in hostess, it's my duty to spread Christmas cheer."

"Oh, is that what you call it today?" He grinned and trailed a finger along her inner thigh. She opened her legs, and he stroked along her slick, hot folds. He loved the way she felt. "Christmas cheer. I'm all for it, babe."

She moved against his finger. Wet and ready. "This was my room when I was in high school."

He so didn't need the amulet to follow this. "Ah, is this one of your fantasies? To have sex at your parents' house in your bed?"

"Uh-huh." Her breath came in short, hard pants. For that matter, so did his.

"Naughty, Giselle. I like you naughty, babe. Did you ever do this with Barry?"

"No. He said he wasn't comfortable doing it here."

"Good." Sam said.

"Did you and Helene…"

"No. It just never came up."

She leaned over him and rimmed the head of his cock with her tongue, flashing him a wanton smile. "Well, I'm glad it's up now."

She rose to her knees and straddled him. Okay, they were moving right along. He grinned as he grasped her hips in his hands, his fingers sinking into the soft flesh. He knew her well enough to know she was thoroughly turned on by the idea of getting it on in her parents' house. Hey, it worked for him. Whatever she wanted. "Here, babe, spread your Christmas cheer."

Giselle eased down until she'd sheathed the tip of his cock in her slick, tight channel. "Is that enough cheer for you?"

"It's a nice start but *more*." The last word turned out to be a groan as she slid all the way down, taking him fully inside her. Sweet, sweet, heaven. His eyes damn near rolled back in his head as she slid up and down him. He'd happily spend the rest of his life playing out her fantasies.

"Marry me," he said.

She paused on the downstroke. "What?"

"Marry me."

She threw her head back and laughed. "Oh, my God, you proposed in mid-stroke."

"Say you'll be mine."

"Let me think about it. I don't want us to rush into anything." She slowly rose up and then plunged back down. "Okay. Yes." He was so damn happy. From now on, whatever they faced, they'd face together. "But you know I'm going to have to come up with some other story. I can't tell people you proposed while we were doing this."

He met her on the downslide with an upward thrust. "You'll come up with something, babe. You've got a great imagination. And I'm pretty fond of your Christmas cheer, too."

Epilogue

Christmas, one year later...

"IN THE ONGOING Randolph family Christmas tradition, I'd like to propose a toast," Giselle's father said, standing at the head of the feast-laden table.

For as long as she could remember, her father had intoned the same thing at the start of their Christmas meal. It was one of her favorite parts.

"To family. And another year of love." It was always the same toast, as well, which worked as far as she was concerned. If it wasn't broke, don't fix it.

Everyone toasted with a glass of zinfandel served in Waterford crystal. Everyone except Giselle, who sipped from her water glass. Across the dining room table, Helene sent her sister a questioning look.

Beside her, Sam clasped her hand in his, his excitement a palpable thing. They shared a smile. The past year had been incredible, better than she'd ever dreamed it could be.

After one very frank, blunt discussion to clear the air, Sam had begun to build new, different relationships with Danny and Helene, that of a brother-in-law rather than ex-husband, former friend, and husband. And Giselle and Helene's relationship had shifted and grown, as well. Oddly enough, when Giselle had stopped treating Helene like a baby sister and more like an adult, Helene had responded by being more mature and less selfish. And Giselle and Sam. She'd thought things couldn't possibly get better, but their relationship had grown deeper and richer. They argued, occasionally they fought, and they'd both had to adjust to living with the other and marriage in general, but in the end it all came back to one thing. They loved.

Giselle cleared her throat. "Sam and I wanted to share something with everyone." It'd been hard not to tell her mother ahead of time, but they'd wanted to wait until now, at Christmas, to tell everyone. "This time next year, there'll be a new family member." She couldn't contain her smile of happiness. She felt as if her joy was pouring out of her face. "We're expecting a baby in June."

At the opposite end of the table from her father, her mother burst into tears. "Oh, honey, I'm so happy." She looked at her husband. "We're going to be grandparents, Ford."

In the meantime, Helene had rounded the table and was laughing and crying and hugging both Sam and Giselle at the same time. "And I'm going to be an aunt."

They were a family.

* * * * *

*Runaway bride Payton Harwell thinks she's hit rock
bottom when she ends up in jail – in Australia!
But then sexy rebel Brody Quinn bails her out and lets
her into his home, his bed, his life. Only Payton's
past isn't as far away as she thinks it is...*

Turn the page for a sneak preview of

The Mighty Quinns: Brody
by Kate Hoffmann

*available from Mills & Boon® Blaze®
in January 2010*

The Mighty Quinns: Brody
by
Kate Hoffmann

Queensland, Australia—June, 2009

HIS BODY ACHED, from the throbbing in his head to the deep, dull pain in his knee. The various twinges in between—his back, his right elbow, the fingers of his left hand—felt worse than usual. Brody Quinn wondered if he'd always wake up with a reminder of the motorcycle accident that had ruined his future or, if someday, all the pain would magically be gone.

Hell, he'd just turned twenty-six and he felt like an old man. Reaching up, he rubbed his forehead, certain of only one thing—he'd spent the previous night sitting on his arse at the Spotted Dog getting himself drunk.

The sound of an Elvis Presley tune drifted through the air and Brody knew exactly where he'd slept it off— the Bilbarra jail. The town's police chief, Angus Embley, was a huge fan of Presley, willing to debate the King's singular place in the world of music with any bloke who dared to argue the point. Right now, Elvis was only exacerbating Brody's headache.

"Angus!" he shouted. "Can you turn down the music?"

Since he'd returned home to his family's cattle station in Queensland, he'd grown rather fond of the accommodations at the local jail. Though he usually ended up behind bars for some silly reason, it saved him the long drive home or sleeping it off in his SUV. "Angus!"

"He's not here. He went out to get some breakfast."

Brody rolled over to look into the adjoining cell, startled to hear a female voice. As he rubbed his bleary eyes, he focused on a slender woman standing just a few feet away, dressed in a pretty, flowered blouse and blue jeans. Her delicate fingers were wrapped around the bars that separated them, her dark eyes intently fixed on his.

"Christ," he muttered, flopping back onto the bed. Now he'd really hit bottom, Brody mused, throwing his arm over his eyes. Getting royally pissed was one thing, but hallucinating a female prisoner was another. He was still drunk.

He closed his eyes, but the image of her swirled in his brain. Odd that he'd conjured up this particular apparition. She didn't really fit his standard of beauty. He usually preferred blue-eyed blondes with large breasts and shapely backsides and long, long legs.

This woman was slim, with deep mahogany hair that fell in a riot of curls around her face and shoulders. By his calculations, she might come up to his chin at best. And her features were…odd. Her lips were almost too lush and her cheekbones too high. And her skin was so pale and perfect that he had to wonder if she ever spent a day in the sun.

"You don't have to be embarrassed. A lot of people talk in their sleep."

Brody sat up. She had an American accent. His fantasy women never had American accents. "What?"

She stared at him from across the cell. "It was mostly just mumbling. And some snoring. And you did mention someone named Nessa."

"Vanessa," he murmured, scanning her features again. She wasn't wearing a bit of makeup, yet she looked as if she'd just stepped out of the pages of one of those fashion magazines Vanessa always had on hand. She had that fresh-scrubbed, innocent, girl-next-door look about her. Natural. Clean. He wondered if she smelled as good as she looked.

Since returning home, there hadn't been a single woman who'd piqued his interest—until now. Though she could be anywhere between sixteen and thirty, Brody reckoned if she was younger than eighteen, she wouldn't be sitting in a jail cell. It was probably safe to lust after her.

"You definitely said Nessa," she insisted. "I remember. I thought it was an odd name."

"It's short for Vanessa. She's a model and that's what they call her." Nessa was so famous, she didn't need a last name, kind of like Madonna or Sting.

"She's your girlfriend?"

"Yes." He drew a sharp breath, then cleared his throat. "No. Ex-girlfriend."

"Sorry," she said with an apologetic shrug. "I didn't mean to stir up bad memories."

"No bad memories," Brody replied, noting the hint of defensiveness in his voice. What the hell did he care what this woman thought of him—or the girls he'd dated? He swung his legs off the edge of the bed, then raked his hands through his hair. "I know why *I'm* here. What are *you* doing in a cell?"

"Just a small misunderstanding," she said, forcing a smile.

"Angus doesn't lock people up for small misunderstandings," Brody countered, pushing to his feet. "Especially not women." He crossed to stand in front of her, wrapping his fingers around the bars just above hers. "What did you do?"

"Dine and dash," she said.

"What?"

Her eyes dropped and a pretty blush stained her cheeks. "I—I skipped out on my bill at the diner down the street. And a few other meals in a few other towns. I guess my life of crime finally caught up with me. The owner called the cops and I'm in here until I find a way to work it off."

He pressed his forehead into the bars, hoping the cool iron would soothe the ache in his head. "Why don't you just pay for what you ate?"

"I would have, but I didn't have any cash. I left an IOU. And I said I'd come back and pay as soon as I found work. I guess that wasn't good enough."

Brody let his hands slide down until he was touching her, if only to prove that she was real and that he wasn't dreaming. "What happened to all your money?" he asked, fixing his attention on her face as he ran his fingers over hers. It seemed natural to touch her, even though she was a complete stranger. Oddly, she didn't seem to mind.

Her breath caught and then she sighed. "It's all gone. Desperate times call for desperate measures. I'm not a dishonest person. I was just really, really hungry."

She had the most beautiful mouth he'd ever seen, her

lips soft and full…perfect for— He fought the urge to pull her closer and take a quick taste, just to see if she'd be…different. "What's your name?"

"Payton," she murmured.

"Payton," he repeated, leaning back to take in details of her body. "Is that your last name or your first?"

"Payton Harwell," she said.

"And you're American?"

"I am."

"And you're in jail," he said, stating the obvious.

She laughed softly and nodded as she glanced around. "It appears I am. At least for a while. Angus told me as soon as he finds a way for me to work off my debt, he'll let me out. I told him I could wash dishes at the diner, but the owner doesn't want me back there. I guess jobs are in short supply around here."

Brody's gaze drifted back to her face—he was oddly fascinated by her features. Had he seen her at a party or in a nightclub in Fremantle, he probably wouldn't have given her a second glance. But given time to appreciate her attributes, he couldn't seem to find a single flaw worth mentioning.

"Quinn!"

Brody glanced over his shoulder and watched as Angus strolled in, his freshly pressed uniform already rumpled after just a few hours of work. "Are you sober yet?"

"You didn't have to lock me up," Brody said, letting go of the bars.

"Brody Quinn, you started a brawl, you broke a mirror and you threw a bleedin' drink in my face, after insulting my taste in music. You didn't give me a choice." Angus braced his hands on his hips. "There'll be a fine. I figure a couple hundred should do it. And you're gonna have to pay for Buddy's mirror." Angus scratched his chin. "And I want a promise you're gonna behave yourself from now on and respect the law. Your brother's here, so pay the fine and you can go."

"Teague is here?" Brody asked.

"No, Callum is waiting. He's not so chuffed he had to make a trip into town."

"I could have driven myself home," Brody said.

"Your buddy Billy tried to take your keys last night. That's what started the fight. He flushed the keys, so Callum brought your spare." Angus reached down and unlocked the cell. "Next time you kick up a stink, I'm holding you for a week. That's a promise."

Brody turned back and looked at Payton. "You can let her out. I'll pay her fine, too."

"First you have to settle up with Miss Shelly over at the coffeeshop and then you have to find this young lady a job. Then, I'll let you pay her fine. Until you do all that, she's gonna be a guest for a bit longer."

"It's all right," Payton said in a cheerful voice. "I'm okay here. I've got a nice place to sleep and regular meals."

Brody frowned as he shook his head. It just didn't feel right leaving her locked up, even if she did want to stay. "Suit yourself," he said, rubbing at the ache in his head.

Payton gave him a little wave, but it didn't ease his qualms. Who was she? And what had brought her to Bilbarra? There were a lot of questions running through his mind without any reasonable answers.

millsandboon.co.uk Community

Join Us!

The Community is the perfect place to meet and chat to kindred spirits who love books and reading as much as you do, but it's also the place to:

- Get the inside scoop from authors about their latest books
- Learn how to write a romance book with advice from our editors
- Help us to continue publishing the best in women's fiction
- Share your thoughts on the books we publish
- Befriend other users

Forums: Interact with each other as well as authors, editors and a whole host of other users worldwide.

Blogs: Every registered community member has their own blog to tell the world what they're up to and what's on their mind.

Book Challenge: We're aiming to read 5,000 books and have joined forces with The Reading Agency in our inaugural Book Challenge.

Profile Page: Showcase yourself and keep a record of your recent community activity.

Social Networking: We've added buttons at the end of every post to share via digg, Facebook, Google, Yahoo, technorati and de.licio.us.

www.millsandboon.co.uk

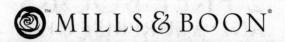

2 FREE BOOKS
AND A SURPRISE GIFT

We would like to take this opportunity to thank you for reading this Mills & Boon® book by offering you the chance to take TWO more specially selected titles from the Blaze® series absolutely FREE! We're also making this offer to introduce you to the benefits of the Mills & Boon® Book Club™—

- **FREE home delivery**
- **FREE gifts and competitions**
- **FREE monthly Newsletter**
- **Exclusive Mills & Boon Book Club offers**
- **Books available before they're in the shops**

Accepting these FREE books and gift places you under no obligation to buy, you may cancel at any time, even after receiving your free books. Simply complete your details below and return the entire page to the address below. You don't even need a stamp!

YES Please send me 2 free Blaze books and a surprise gift. I understand that unless you hear from me, I will receive 3 superb new books every month, including a 2-in-1 book priced at £4.99 and two single books priced at £3.19 each, postage and packing free. I am under no obligation to purchase any books and may cancel my subscription at any time. The free books and gift will be mine to keep in any case.

Ms/Mrs/Miss/Mr _____ Initials _____

_____

Surname _____

Address _____

_____

_____ Postcode _____

Send this whole page to: Mills & Boon Book Club, Free Book Offer, FREEPOST NAT 10298, Richmond, TW9 1BR